# HUNTING STRATEGY

Book 2 of the Thunderstrike Diaries

## WENDY METCALFE

# CHAPTER ONE

PREDATORBOTS AREN'T SUPPOSED TO feel scared. I'm a fierce female lion, and I'm not supposed to get anxious. But I was as *Thunderstrike* approached his downjump at Vasant Station.

I sat in Strike's control room, in my usual space beside the captain's seat, and my body was tense. Bahar looked down at me, and trailed her dark fingers through my neck fur. "Relax, Snap," she said.

She wasn't relaxed, so why should she expect me to be? I could smell her scent of uncertainty, laced through with a ribbon of fear. Humans always forgot that I could smell their emotions.

"I hope Chan didn't tell anyone we were coming here," I said.

"I didn't tell the group anything about our plans." Strike spoke up, over the ship's com. "I... had a sense she wasn't trustworthy before she made that report."

'That report' was the file Chan had tried to send to Olianna Station Security. It would've exposed our unofficial Special Investigations Unit as working against the Collective President. It would've got us killed.

Strike and nineteen other machine intelligences had killed Chan, and prevented her report getting through. But we didn't know if she'd told anyone else about the Unit before then.  We didn't know what we'd face when we downjumped here.

"Downjump in four… three… two… one…"

As usual, Strike cut off his com a microsecond before transition.  He delighted in playing games like that, showing off how good his control of his shipbody was.  Strike was a sapient machine intelligence, and he was just as smart and sneaky and proud and emotional as any human I've met.  He was also my best friend in all the universe.

Bahar's scent spiked with fear again.  It did nothing for my worries.

Through the viewport I saw the greys, blues, and dull reds of hyperspace morph into pure black.  The pressure wave rippling down my flanks confirmed the transition.  We were safely back in normal space.

Whether we were safe was another matter.

"Receiving scan plot now," Strike said as it came up on the screens.

It took me a moment to work out that no-one was shooting at us.  Nobody seemed to be coming towards us either.  It looked like we might get safely into dock this time.

"I've just received docking assignment from station," Strike said.  His voice was calm.  "We're on Level 2, berth 2231.  It's an ordinary Starnavy assignment."

"So far, so good," Bahar replied.

"Goren's just contacted me. He says the station is quiet, and we should be safe here." Goren was an admin machine intelligence at Vasant, and part of the Unit.

"That would be nice," Bahar said. She'd nearly been kidnapped on our last trip ashore, at Revecca Station. I'd had to bite her kidnapper's arm to rescue her.

"Why don't you two get some sleep," Strike said. "We're fifteen hours from dock."

"Good idea," Bahar replied. She levered herself out of her seat. I got to my paws and shook my pelt. I was tired, but whether I would sleep well was another question.

Strike let us out of the control room. I slept in the First Officer's suite, Bahar had the Captain's quarters opposite. Strike opened the door to my rooms and I settled into my large cat bed, smoothing the wrinkles out of my blankets with my paws.

Strike had come under attack recently, and I was still dealing with the fallout from that. I'd had to make some really scary decisions, and do some really scary things. It had affected all of us, and it had made me more tired than I should be.

I turned over on my side and curled up my legs. The blankets in my bed were soft, and laced with comforting scents.

*Sweet dreams, Snap*, Strike said just before sleep took me.

I woke as Strike was entering his line-up for docking. I'd slept for 5.6 hours. Not enough to feel totally rested, but not as bad as I'd feared. Strike fed me in my room, with a large haunch of printer-produced falacca meat. I was hungry, and attacked it greedily.

*Are we still safe?* I asked over our feed line.

*So far. Goren's analysed the loyalties on Vasant. He says he can't find any traitors here.*

*We didn't think Chan was a traitor.*

*I've been researching her recent movements. She got a new captain half a Standard before she... I think he turned her sympathies back to the Collective.*

*Oh.* If you thought machine intelligences were purely rational beings, think again. Human psychs had identified something they labelled 'machine intelligence attachment syndrome'. Humans would just call it falling in love.

I finished my meal, leaving only a few stringy bits I couldn't break up. Strike insisted on printing authentic meat, but then he complained about the mess I made when I left behind the gristle.

*Let me clean up, messy cat,* he said. *Go to the control room.*

I got to my paws and shook my pelt, settling it into order as Strike's clean-up drone entered my quarters. *Is Bahar awake?* I asked.

*Up, and fretting,* Strike replied. The exasperation I heard in his voice was softened by affection.  That was business as usual.

He opened the doors for me, and I entered the control room. Bahar was slumped in the captain's seat.  She'd unbound her hair today, and it billowed out in a curly black cloud around her head. But unlike our last visit ashore, she wasn't wearing fine tribal dress.  She'd opted for a drab wardrobe of combat pants and shirt in dark shades of blue.  That told me she was still bothered by her kidnap.

She looked down as I came to sit beside her seat, and trailed her fingers over my neck.  "Sleep well, Snap?" she asked.

"Not long enough," I said.  "I don't understand why I'm always so tired."

She stroked me again.  "That's just your body dealing with all the crap we've faced recently."

I hoped she was right.  On Olianna I'd had to have some remedial code patches installed to stop my implanted processors trying to access data which my memories no longer held.  My body felt different now, and sometimes it still unsettled me.

"How far out are we?" I asked.  I could read Strike's nav displays, but I couldn't translate what I saw there into time estimates.

"Four and a half hours," he said, using the wildly inaccurate estimates Bahar preferred.

"I wonder what we'll find this time," she said.

"Hopefully… Alert!" Strike's voice was sharp. "Traffic Control's just warned me that a ship's off line, and headed our way."

"Knew it couldn't be that easy," Bahar grumbled. "Are they raiders?"

"We're about to find out," Strike replied.

# CHAPTER TWO

"*THUNDERSTRIKE*, HAZARD WARNING." The voice from Traffic Control sounded strained. "The liner *Starveil* is headed your way. It's believed they've lost helm control. Divert to these co-ordinates."

"Acknowledged," Strike said. "Diverting now."

The display showed Strike firing thrusters in a complex pattern, turning us off our approach line. The nav display showed a scatter of moving dots. Those were other ships also being moved out of range.

"Defensive suites on-line," Strike announced.

That meant he'd activated his anti-scan net. It was becoming a routine occurrence to be approached by ships on our way in to stations. The last time one had got really close it had been trying to scan us.

At the time, we didn't know why. We didn't think it had succeeded, but after the Chan incident now I wasn't so sure. The more I thought about it, the more convinced I was that someone knew Strike had a Predatorbot aboard, and was scanning for me.

*External coms shut down to Traffic Control link*, Strike said over our private feed. *I'm not getting caught like that again.*

I couldn't think of anything to say to that. Bahar's scent now had a touch of fear to it.  She thought this wasn't an innocent move.  I still wasn't sure.

The approaching ship wasn't coming straight for us.  It kept making what looked like random course changes.  That would fit with a loss of helm control.

"Advisory," the Traffic Controller sent.  "The *Starveil* has asked for tug assistance.  Ship will be remaining at current co-ordinates for the next three local hours."  That meant they'd given up trying to fly the ship.  "Recalculating your approach line now.  Thank you for your patience."

"So it's a genuine failure?" Bahar asked.

"It looks like it.  I haven't detected any attempts to scan or attack us," Strike replied.  "And… receiving recalculated line now.  Sorry, people.  It's going to take us another hour to get into dock."

Strike's estimate was right.  We docked normally, and no other problems came up on our way in.

"I've filed my navigation report with Station," Strike said.  "Traffic Control confirms the incident was a genuine loss of helm control."

"It's worrying that it occurred on a liner," Bahar said.  "With all those passengers aboard."

"It's a Nexus Starribbon ship."

"Ah, right."

I knew what Bahar meant by that comment. The shipline was a low-cost carrier. Nobody had ever been able to prove that they skimped on ship maintenance, but they were rumoured to do the absolute legal minimum. If I was a civilian traveller it isn't a shipline I'd choose.

Humans have very dubious morals sometimes. I've never understood this need to grab as much credit as you can during your lifetime. I can see the benefits of not being poor. Being able to eat good food when you need it is definitely a good thing. So is having somewhere safe and comfortable to lay your head at the end of the day. But amassing credits just to buy shiny bits of metal to hang around your neck, that I've never understood.

"All connections made to station. Beginning refuel now," Strike said, cutting into my musing.

That was one of the reasons why our bogus Unit needed to look like it was an official part of the Starnavy. Strike had to get fuel and supplies from somewhere.

Technically, Strike was a rogue, but there are degrees of rogue. There are people who want to destroy everybody and everything connected to the Collective. He's not that kind of person. He's the kind of rogue who rights injustices created by misuse of power. He also tries to stop greedy planet-trashers.

Strike calls what we do morally grey. That's a weird phrase.

How can a concept have a colour?

"Goren's sent me a situation report," Strike said. "He tells me it's still calm on-station. He's put in a request for a meeting about Chan with you, Snap."

"Why me?" I asked.

"I think he's worried about the attack on me. He wants you to brief him and the other Unit machine intelligences here."

"I thought that was over," I said. My voice was sharp.

"I could tell him no," Strike offered. "We could put in a written report from here."

"They're scared, aren't they?" I asked.

Strike paused for 6.7 seconds. "Yes," he said softly. "Every machine intelligence in the Unit is scared by that attack on me. They're all wondering if they're going to be the next target."

"It can't happen like that again. I don't have my behaviour module any more."

"They don't know that's how the attack happened. I haven't told anyone I have a Predatorbot aboard."

"So you want me to go ashore and show myself to strangers, to risk potential danger just to soothe a few machine intelligences?"

"To soothe two hundred and sixteen machine intelligences," Strike replied.

That... was a lot of people. My mind flicked back to the

conversation I'd had with Strike after Chan's death. We'd talked about the greater good.

This was one of those situations. I was going to have to face my fears and go on-station. I owed that to every machine intelligence in the Unit.


This time, I changed the camouflage on my armour to display a garish folk-art daisy pattern in bright yellow and orange on a green background. I reckoned that anyone looking for a Predatorbot wouldn't look twice at a petbot with such a hideous coat. What did Strike call it? Hiding in plain sight.

Bahar laughed when she saw it. "I have just the accessory for that," she said. She disappeared into her quarters, and returned wearing a bright yellow-and-orange large glass daisy flower on a thong. She saw me looking at it, and said, "I know. It isn't me. It's one of my mother's pieces. She had hideous taste in jewellery."

I knew Bahar's mother had been dead for five Standards. This jewellery was one of Bahar's mementoes.

"It jars against your clothes," Strike said. "You should wear something brighter."

Bahar shook her head. "I don't want to draw attention to myself after our last outing. I… I have to get over that, don't I?"

"You do," Strike agreed.

"Okay. Back in a minute," she said, and headed for her quarters.

We'd both been scared by the attack on Revecca Station. We'd always thought that Bahar would be safe with me by her side. I couldn't fully extend my armour when I went ashore, because that exposed the gun ports on my shoulders and forehead. Nobody would believe I was an innocent petbot then. And my safety relied on everyone believing I was an innocent petbot.

So we were both scared of getting hurt on station again. Bahar wasn't the only one who needed to get over that. I did too.

She reappeared, wearing a plain yellow linen shirt and loose dark green trousers. Their colours were bright, but the clothes were faded and creased.

"Perfect," Strike said. "Goren's promised to track you through the station to the conference room. Off you go."

The firmness in his voice got through to Bahar. She straightened her spine, and took in a breath.

"Okay, Snap. Let's do this," she said.

# CHAPTER THREE

BAHAR AND I CAME onto the dock at shift change. It was station Second Shift, and from out of nowhere the dock was suddenly full of people. Some were Starnavy, but many were techs in station's uniform, and there was a good scattering of people in civvy dress among them.

None of them stood out like we did. We were bright spots in a sea of darker colours. We certainly weren't blending in.

Bahar was too tense to look like a trooper on vacation. She smelled anxious too. I secured a private feed line with her and said, *Relax. We have to look like we're on leave.*

I saw her shoulders drop, and she took in a long, slow, breath. *We're too visible*, she said over our feed line.

*That's the idea. We're hiding in plain sight, remember?*

Goren cut in on our feed. *I'm tracking you. There's no trouble on-station anywhere near you.*

Did that mean there was trouble elsewhere? I didn't want to know.

Our route to the conference suite took us down one level and around a quarter of station's ring. The hallways were still busy after shift change, but nobody bothered us. I even managed to move through the crowds without anyone bumping into my nose.  That was a big bonus.

We reached the conference wing and Bahar turned into the wide hallway which led to the bigger rooms.  As we approached our destination she stiffened-up.  *That's Kemel Tazzu*, she said.  Her anxious smell increased.

*He's out of uniform*, Strike replied.  *Goren told me he did leave the Starnavy.*

*It's odd he should be here*, Bahar said.

*Goren, do you know anything about him?* I asked.

*Relax.  He's part of our conference admin team.  He looks after logistics here.*

Right.  That was handy cover for anyone wanting to hack into conference conversations.

*We'll make things secure.  Don't worry*, Goren said.

We reached the conference room, and when I walked in I was surprised to see people in it.  Most of the local and on-station Unit machine intelligences had sent physical avatars.  Over a hundred of them sat there.  I hadn't expected that.  Bahar sat down at the table facing the tiered semi-circular rows of seats.  I came to sit beside her.  She smelled nervous, shot through with a spike of fear.

"Welcome, Bahar, Snap," a voice said from the room's nodes. "I am Solana, and I'm moderating this meeting.  We'll be using machine intelligence security protocols to secure our lines in.

Sorry about the noise."

Bahar leaned back in her seat, trying to relax. "No problem. I'm used to it." I saw several of the avatars smile at that.

"We're establishing off-site links now," Solana said.

At the far end of the room, the wallscreen lit. A series of screeches and whistles filled the room. Tiles displaying the Unit members' avatars appeared. As the wall filled up with images I began to fret again about the scale of this meeting.

Chan's betrayal was still too recent. Too raw. I worried that somebody here might be the next Chan. And that, this time, the betrayal might succeed.

# CHAPTER FOUR

I FACED THE ASSEMBLED AVATARS, and felt more nervous than I'd ever done in my life.

"My name is Snap, and I am a Predatorbot," I said.

A ripple of conversation ran through the room. I waited until it finished. "I am *Thunderstrike's* emergency storage for his core. It is where he hid while I dealt with the code attack on him."

"But how could you hold a complete core?" Goren asked.

"Strike implanted extra memories in me for that contingency," I replied.

The ripple of conversation was louder this time, and I wasn't sure that everyone approved of that. They'd like what I said next even less.

"I… was also the vector for the code attack on Strike."

"What?" Goren snarled. "You attacked him?"

"Not knowingly. Would I be standing here in front of you confessing to that if I'd planned it? Would I be risking your anger and the danger of harm if I'd intended to hurt my best friend in all the universe?"

I raised my head and gave them my fierce predator glare, sweeping my gaze from one side of the seated avatars to the other.  The angry mutters died.  I watched each group stiffen up and look away from me as I engaged their gazes.  Being a deadly killing machine had its uses sometimes.

"Snap also found all the hostile code which took over *Thunderstrike's* shipbody," Bahar said.  "She did a complete system check of that shipbody, and found and destroyed every piece of that malware."  She sounded calm, but I could smell her fear.  Bahar was very afraid.

"Then she transferred me back to my shipbody."  Strike spoke up at last.  "If she hadn't done that, I would be dead.  Snap saved my life."

Now the conversations in the room were louder, but their tone was lighter.  The feeling of hostility towards me was fading.

"The code attack was launched through Snap's behaviour module," Bahar said.

"The behaviour module that's killed so many Predatorbots?" Goren asked.  So he at least knew the history of the Programme.

"Yes," I said.  "Strike removed my kill switch when I joined his crew.  He left the module in my body then because he said the risk of injury to me if he removed it was high.

"The attacker used a Teams Link coms circuit in that module to enter my systems.  They attacked my behaviour module with malware first, so that I didn't know I was downloading hostile code.  Then they used me as the vector to send their malware to

*Thunderstrike*."

I saw several of the avatars shiver.  Bahar had been right to insist on detailing the attack.  They were scared by it.  Strike had said they would be.

"We have never heard of a machine intelligence transferring their core like that before," Solana said.  Her voice was soft.  I wasn't sure if I heard jealousy there.  I'd detected an undercurrent of hostility towards Bahar and me when we arrived, but now it was gone.  Bahar sensed it too.  Her body relaxed, and her fear smell died down.

"Snap no longer has her behaviour module," she said.  "Strike removed it.  He also removed the substantial network of filament connections which had grown into Snap's brain."

"That's…" Solana couldn't find the right word.

"Monstrous?" Bahar suggested.  "The whole Predatorbot Programme is a monstrous idea.  None of you carry kill switches."

I saw some of the avatars shiver.  I was glad the ships had sent them.  Reading their body language, I could see we'd frightened them.

Bahar hadn't wanted that.  Strike had.  He'd wanted to make it clear how dangerous the attack on him had been.

"We didn't know if removing those filaments from Snap's brain would cause neural damage.  We risked losing the Snap we love," Bahar said. "But for the safety of all of us, that surgery had to be done."

The quiet in the room was total. Nobody fidgeted, or whispered anything. The avatars sat stiff and still, processing Bahar's words. I could smell her nervousness.

The silence stretched out for 3.2 minutes, then Solana broke it.

"Was the surgery… successful?" she asked.

"It was," I replied. "The vector for that attack no longer exists in my body."

"I meant are you okay," she said.

"The surgery didn't damage my brain."

Again there was that silence; for 3.4 minutes this time. I don't know why I hadn't just said yes. I think I wanted to make them squirm.

That… isn't helpful. Stop this, Snap. These are your allies. Or they're supposed to be.

"I think we all owe Snap a huge debt of gratitude for keeping every one of us safe," Solana said.

The avatars rose to their feet and clapped their hands. It was totally unexpected, and it startled me.

I moved back to Bahar's seat, and she reached a hand down and stroked my neck. Her scent was finally calm. "A standing ovation," she said. "Good. Very good. Much better than I'd expected."

When the noise died down Solana said, "This attack on Strike has brought the future of the Unit into focus.  I believe we can't go on as we are.

"This is the first time we have gathered so many members together for a meeting, and doing so is not without risk, but I think it was essential.  So far, we've operated as a loose collection of people.  I think it's time we got serious.  I am proposing that we draw up a Charter, which we all sign up to. That should concentrate our minds on what we stand for."

"I'd hesitated to suggest that," Strike said, "but after Chan's betrayal I would welcome the reassurance."

Again there was silence in the room.  It was broken by Solana.  "I've opened a file and inserted some suggested text. Let's talk about what we want to sign up to."

It took 3.7 hours to agree the text of the Charter.  I hadn't expected such a long session.  Humans argued like that, I didn't expect machine intelligences to.

I wondered how the humans who worked alongside these contacts would take this development.  Whether someone would find out about the Charter.  Whether it would prompt another hysterical outbreak of 'AIs are taking over the universe'.

The first panic like that was a century ago, and resulted in the deaths of many machine intelligences. They've learned caution since then, learned not to show their power. I'm sure they'll find a way to manage this.

When the meeting ended Strike wanted us to come straight back to his shipbody. He sounded anxious, but he said nothing was wrong.

Goren confirmed that our route back to the dock was clear, so we made our way to the lifts and went up one level.

We were between shifts, and the hallways were much quieter than when we came on-station. Bahar played with her pendant as she walked, running her fingers over the glass. She was lost in thought, and I didn't disturb her. Her scent was calm.

We came onto the dock three berths down from *Thunderstrike*. The dock was quiet too. As we passed the berth next to *Thunderstrike's* a Station Security skimmer hurtled down the dock, its horn blaring, startling Bahar into releasing a spike of fear scent. By the time we reached Strike's berth the skimmer was nowhere in sight.

"Wonder what emergency they were going to?" she asked.

"I'm sure Strike will be able to tell us." The Security call-out had bothered me. Was this another attempt to hurt Strike? I needed to get aboard and talk to him.

As we approached the berth the lockout gate opened. That was good. Last time we'd returned to Strike from on-station he'd not let us in automatically. That was just after he'd discovered what Chan had done.

We strode up the ramp and Strike opened the outer airlock door for us. "Come to the control room," he said as we stepped into the airlock. "We need to talk."

He brought us up in the lift to Deck Two, and Bahar said, "I'm going to go change first." She opened the door to her quarters and disappeared inside. I went to the control room.

"So, we have a Charter," Strike said as I settled down to wait for Bahar.

"Yes. This thing is getting really serious now."

"So is the level of corruption in the Collective," Strike replied. "I've received evidence of rigged Colony Governor elections on six Outliers in the Lidwina Cluster."

"That's not unusual," I said. Our last planetary landing on Reeva had got us involved with a corrupt Colony Chairperson.

"True, but the fact that these are the six closest planets to each other is unusual. Ebony is concerned about it. She thinks there's a new organisation emerging out there."

Oh, right. Ebony was the machine intelligence of the civilian courier *Black Velvet.* She was a brilliant political strategist and had taken on a political advisory role for the Unit.

"If Ebony's worried, then we need to take note," Bahar said, entering the control room then. She settled into the captain's seat and let out a long sigh. "I'm glad that meeting's over. I wasn't sure we'd get away with it."

"I'm not entirely sure we did get away with it," Strike said.

He sent video to the wallscreen. "This is the dock outside. Timestamp is twenty-five minutes before you arrived."

A lone figure in a faded Vasant Station uniform walked down the dock towards Strike's berth. He was carrying a hand unit, and glancing down at it as he walked.

"That's Kemel Tazzu. And he's scanning for something," Bahar said. Her anxiety-scent was back.

"Correct. I rode the scanner's outputs back to read its controls. He was searching for data on my defensive suites."

"Did he…"

"All he got was gibberish, Snap. Watch what happens next."

A single-seat personnel pod whizzed around the curve of the dock. It stopped close to Strike's berth and a figure in full armour with helmet visor down leapt out. Xe was carrying a large energy weapon.

Xe pumped five bursts into Kemel's unprotected body, then turned around and returned to the pod. Bahar's scent spiked to fear as the pod shot off, leaving Kemel's dead body in a heap on the deck. The whole incident had lasted only minutes.

"I picked up no audio between them," Strike said. "I don't know what the context for this murder is."

"Station Security are bound to ask you what you know about it," Bahar said. She smelled anxious again.

"Why would I know anything? My monitoring only extends as far as my lockout gate."

Bahar laughed. "Yeah, sure."

"I've sent Goren the vid, but I'm keen to avoid getting tangled up in an official investigation. I've put in a departure request. And… we've just been assigned an immediate outbound lane."

"Goren fixed it for us," Bahar said.

I thought that was probably right. There was no certainty that Kemel intended anything hostile towards us, but it was odd that we'd bumped into him in the conference suite earlier and then he'd ended up dead outside Strike's berth.

"Firing thrusters to take us outbound now," Strike announced. "Chatter with Traffic Control is normal."

So they weren't going to stop us leaving. But we were running away from a station – again. This was getting to be a bad habit.

# CHAPTER FIVE

STRIKE DECIDED TO MAKE for Hasana Station. It was on the fringe of the Lidina Cluster, and a place we'd visited before.

I had a very dark thought about the attack on the dock as Strike made his way out from it. What if Kemel's killer was an avatar? Perhaps even one of those present in the meeting I'd spoken at? No, why should it be? Unless Kemel had discovered the Unit and told on us.

I didn't think that was likely. I thought it was far more probable that he'd cheated someone who'd taken exception to his double-dealing. Hopefully we'd never need to know. I had to remind myself that not everything which happened was about us.

Strike used his Starnavy codes to strip the sats of  any advisories as he made his way out to the jump point. There was nothing happening locally, but a Watch Order had been issued for Jaran. Jaran was one of the planets served by the Zurrial Triangle stations, and was rumoured to be harbouring this new dissident organisation. It was calling itself Outlier Action. So it was more than mere rumour that trouble might be brewing out there.

I didn't rate the Starnavy's data analysis skills. They did lots of what Strike called combat modelling, working out how many ships they'd need to win a battle. It never ended up the way they planned.

Strike had read their analyses. They put their failures down to poor tactics, or bad decisions by individual captains. They never considered that machine intelligences had acted.

The Unit had played a big role in decisions not to engage in several potential conflicts. We'd moved ships away from areas of tension, so that the Starnavy didn't have the resources to mount a quick offensive. They'd had to do the much harder thing and talk to the people they disliked.

But now we were going towards an area of tension. The last thing we needed was to get called up for combat there.

I slept for 9.6 hours, and woke just before Strike took us into jump.

*Stay in your bed while I take us through, sleepyhead*, he said over our feed line. His voice was soft with affection.

I yawned, and stretched out my legs. *Then be quick about it. I'm hungry.*

*You're always hungry.*

*You eat too. All the time.* The bickering was starting to get silly now.

*If I didn't, I couldn't keep you safe.  Jump in three... two... one... Insertion complete,* Strike said. *What do you want to eat?*

I asked for a breast of yivant.  They were big, flightless birds from Faruz, and they were extinct in the wild.  Humans had hunted them for their meat, and eaten all their eggs.

The meat was very sweet, and I only ate it as an occasional treat.  Strike said its sugar content was right at the limit of tolerance for my stomach.

Strike knows a lot about my body.  Yes, his medsystem needs that knowledge, but Strike the person doesn't.  It's another way he shows that he cares about me.

I ate, then left my quarters to let Strike clear up after me.  He let me into the control room, and for once Bahar wasn't there.

"She's down in the cryobay, doing her ritual inspection." Strike's voice betrayed his exasperation at her.

Strike is a Human Collective Starnavy frigate, and he carries twenty troops.  They spend a lot of their time in coldsleep in Strike's cryobay.  Bahar always fusses about them, and does a ritual inspection of the cryopods twice a day when she's aboard. She'd be better off doing some exercise on the machines in the med bay to work out her tension.

I'm too heavy for a running machine.  That was one thing the Predatorbot Programme didn't have.  Instead they'd teased us with lures to chase.  That was until we got uplifted and realised how stupid that was.

Bahar appeared in the control room an hour later, and plopped into her seat. "I wonder what we'll find at this destination," she said. "I hope we don't downjump into war." She smelled low-level anxious.

I hoped Nyla and her sisters weren't anywhere near this rumoured tension. Nyla Vatan had been a neuroscientist at the Predatorbot Programme – until she'd discovered we had kill switches installed in our behaviour modules. When they recruited her they hadn't told her the dark truth about the Programme.

When she found out, she smuggled me onto *Thunderstrike*. Then she outed the Programme and went on the run. We've been looking for her and her four sisters for a Standard.

We found one of those sisters, Fia, on Reeva, and sent her back to her colony on Davion. Strike is working with contacts in the Unit to make Davion a safe haven. Our plan is to rescue Nyla and her other sisters and take them all there until fallout from outing the Programme passes.

Several prominent Administrators lost their careers as a result of Nyla making the Programme's existence public. They all want her dead. We aren't going to let that happen.

The time in jump passed in the usual routine of eating,

sleeping, and prowling around the ship. Strike sent me down to the vehicle bay to do an inspection of the hulls of his two small shuttles.

It wasn't entirely make-work. His bots did regular inspections, but I could sense things they discounted. Weird as it seems, I can smell whether a hull is sound or not.

Strike used my enhanced senses to do regular inspections of his vehicles. I didn't object. I was the one who had to ride in them, so I had a stake in seeing they were safe.

I didn't find any problems this time, but the exercise filled a few hours.


By the time we neared emergence Bahar had taken out every EVA suit from its locker in the storage bay and checked it over, walked through all the hydroponics compartments, and done an unnecessary rearrangement of items stored in the rec area.

We'd reached the usual level of terminal boredom by the time Strike announced that we were nearing downjump.

Downjump was always a scary moment. There was the ever-present threat of raiders, but we also had a different threat. Ships were required to have their ID running at all times while they were within a station's admin area. Not broadcasting immediately you downjumped got you labelled as a rogue. But broadcasting a Collective Starnavy ID immediately brought you to the attention of the local Commander, and put you at risk of local deployment.

So Strike always had half a dozen alias IDs to use, and changed them regularly. He posed as a small carrier, and was usually ignored because he was too small to be useful.

Using an alias had another function. It notified the local Unit machine intelligences that we were there. We got data downloads from contacts on the station, and advance warnings of any trouble, long before we got into dock.

Bahar joined me in the control room just before downjump. She looked relaxed, and that surprised me. So did her calm scent.

"Commencing downjump now," Strike said, and counted us down.

I felt the usual ripple of transition run down my flanks as we emerged from hyperspace.

"Uh-oh," Strike said. "Warnings issued. Hostile action out on the far side of station. Not sure… Ah, hostiles are inbound. They're trying to attack the station. Abir's just contacted me. We're requested to go help defend it."

"On whose orders?" Bahar asked.

"He's part of Security, but he's requesting on behalf of the Unit. Which means I have a free choice of actions."

"So are we getting involved?" Bahar asked.

"They've just hit station.  They've caused a minor hull breach on Level Two.  Yes, we're getting involved.  Going in now."

# CHAPTER SIX

*THUNDERSTRIKE'S* POSITION ON THE nav plot changed. He was pouring on the power to get there fast. I watched him alter his course, coming up under the station to its far side.

"We're joining *Nightlance* and *Blackthunder* to defend station," Strike said.

Now I could see the two ships labelled on the nav display. Strike was coming up in the middle of them. "Shields up. Engaging now," he said.

The battle lasted three shipboard hours. The raiders got in another hit on the station before *Thunderstrike* and *Nightlance* together destroyed their last ship. They were determined but not very skilled foes, and we'd managed to finish the engagement without sustaining any damage.

"We're getting a sitrep from Abir," Strike said. "He says Level Two has a small hull breach. Three sections are locked down and in vacuum. They're sending repair crews out now. They're asking us to stay out here and provide a defensive cordon while they do the repairs."

"In case other raiders come in," Bahar replied. She still had a trace of anxiety-smell, and I could scent the sourness of her body sweat.

"Exactly. I've agreed to that. Sorry, people. We'll be a while longer getting into dock."

When we eventually docked it was Hasana Station's Fourth Shift shift change, and the dock was busy. Jaspelix, one of the Unit machine intelligences based here, wanted to meet face to face with us. Bahar was nervous about going on-station, but Strike thought we should go. There were things contacts would only say face to face. And Jaspelix's request had the feeling of an order to it.

This time, Bahar kept on her drab dark blue combat fatigues. Here, that would almost make her stand out. The nearby planet Cassundri housed a universe-famous creatives' colony, and some of that colour and flavour spilled over onto Hasana Station. There were galleries and workshops here, and a sizeable Creative Quarter where all manner of colourful and weird forms of creativity could be bought.

I didn't get a lot of the weirder stuff, where people were 'pushing the boundaries'. Bahar said most humans didn't either. She said the weird stuff came and went, like it was the fashion of the Standard. When it came down to it, people preferred their art not to fry their brains. And maybe to bring a little more beauty into the universe too.

We wove our way through the crowds. To add to the crush, the troop carrier *Manifest Destiny* had just arrived, and was spilling its crew all over the dock. At least if anyone was tracking us that would make things harder.

We went up to Level One, to the commercial quarter where Jaspelix worked. We didn't go to the offices he was housed in. We met his avatar at a swanky café half-way round the ring from there. Starshimmer's was a galaxy-wide chain of businesses, and all its places were spacious and multi-levelled. This one was a café/bar with widely-spaced tables, and favoured by people who wanted to put up sound screens and not be overheard.

Jaspelix's avatar took the form of a Polldi. Bahar called them lizards. She said they were descended from reptiles, and at some point they'd learned to walk on their back pair of legs. Their front pair had become hands. The avatar sported beautiful iridescent turquoise scales which glittered in the café's lights.

"Welcome, Bahar, Snap," he said when we reached his table. "Join me." He flashed his ebony claws, showing off their elegant curves.

Bahar sat down opposite him, and I settled by her side. She ordered lunch, and when the serverdrone had delivered it Jaspelix said, "I am putting up a sound shield." I saw Bahar stiffen as the shield went up. My fur stood on end, and I shook my body to settle it.

"We are seeing some trouble in this sector recently," he said. "We are the third station to be attacked this Standard."

"Why?" Bahar asked. A spike of anxiety laced her calm scent.

"These people are from a group calling themselves Outlier Action. They are trying to build a power base in the Outliers. They asked Hasana Station to join them. We refused. Hence the attack."

"So they're getting to be a serious threat?" Bahar asked.

"A threat which is steadily growing," Jaspelix said. "But that is not the reason why I dragged you onto the station. I know that you are looking for Nyla Vatan and her sisters."

I stiffened-up at the name, and Bahar put a soothing hand on my neck. "We are," she said. Another spike of anxiety-scent came from her.

"We have had a fairly recent sighting of Rhian," Jaspelix said. "It was a Standard ago. At that time, she was working on Dorkas, relocating fire leopards. Dorkas is close to Krenna space, and some ships and humans working out there have disappeared recently. The Starnavy is noticing increased tension along the border with the Krenna."

He paused for a moment, then added, "We have also heard that the Starnavy is shutting down supply runs to the Outliers."

"That's monstrous!" Bahar snarled. "The Collective's

Assembly encouraged people to relocate there, to solve their overpopulation problem.  And now they're leaving them to starve?"

"Sadly, I believe that is what is happening."

*We've got to get back onto the Central Spine*, Strike said in our feed.  Before I could object he added, *Rhian will have moved on from Dorkas by now.  Relocation projects are short.*

*I agree*, Bahar said.  *So where are we going next?*

*Pekado Station, of course*, Strike replied.  *Just as soon as your get yourselves back aboard my shipbody.*

# CHAPTER SEVEN

"WE COULD DO A SUPPLY run to Iwan," Bahar suggested.

Jaspelix blinked his double-lidded eyes. "Now that is a good idea. I could arrange it so you do an official supply run out there. Once you arrive, you would drop off the roster again and be free to go where you need."

"That's an excellent suggestion," Bahar said. "We need to talk to Strike about it, but I expect he'll agree."

"Our latest data shows no problems at Pekado," Jaspelix said.

"Is there anything else you can tell us?" Bahar asked.

"I have been assigned to investigate Chan's actions."

My head came up, and I stared at him. Bahar reached down a hand to stroke my neck. "What do you know?" I asked.

"She changed captains half a Standard before the attack on *Thunderstrike*. She dropped out of Unit contacts shortly after. I think she got attachment syndrome very badly."

Bahar snorted. "Why do psychologists keep calling it that? She fell in love with her captain."

"I believe you are right. Those relationships are unreliable."

Bahar laughed. "Don't tell me. I'm a sex-repulsed aromantic asexual. I don't understand them either."

"Oh. That does make you rather different from most

humans," Jaspelix said.

"It sure does," she replied. I heard the undertone of anger in her voice. Bahar had grown tired of defending her sexuality. She said aromantic asexual people had always experienced hostility.

"The big news is that Chan had a Predatorbot on her crew," Jaspelix said.

"Oh." Bahar looked down at me. I'd stiffened-up again.

So that's how my Teams Link circuit had triggered. The Predatorbot had sent the code which opened the circuit. Chan had used the Predatorbot as the vector to send over her malware.

Rage rose in me. We'd been used as tools yet again. And Chan's actions had resulted in us killing that Predatorbot. I would never forgive her for that.

Chan was dead. That was the past. I needed to leave it behind me, before anger and grief swallowed me up.

Jaspelix didn't have any more useful information for us, and when Bahar had finished her meal Strike said we should come back to his shipbody. He said station's hull breach had been repaired, but the affected sections were still airing-up. No other trouble had erupted here, but I detected a note of worry in his voice.

My thoughts were roiling all the way back to his dock. I was trying to stuff down my anger, but it wasn't working.  It wasn't just against Chan.  It was against the Predatorbot who was part of that attack too.  Who must've told Chan about the Teams Link circuit, and offered to use it to attack me.

That might not be true, I conceded.  If the Predatorbot had been forced to reveal that circuit, if Chan had used its pain circuit to force it to do what she wanted…

What was that expression Bahar used?  Clutching at straws, that was it.  She'd had to explain that one to me.  Yes, I was desperate to find a reason why we were attacked.  A reason which didn't include being betrayed by my own kind.


The dock was quiet, and Strike let us aboard as normal. "We're about to be invaded by Logistics people," he said.  "It would be best if they didn't see Snap."

"Do you think they're looking out for us?" I asked.

"I suspect everyone has standing orders to report sightings of Predatorbots.  So keep out of the way, okay?"

"I'll go to my room," I said as Strike brought us up in the lift. He was seriously worried about me being discovered.  This wasn't the time to push back against his fretting.

He let me into my room, and fed me while Bahar changed into her Starnavy uniform.  Then she went down to talk to the loaders who were filling our holds with medical supplies and machinery parts.  What did Strike call that?  Schmoozing, that was it.

Strike sent me the video from the holds.  Bahar was talking to the loaders about the situation in the Outliers.  A little careful probing by her had them confirming that supply runs were being scaled back.  So the Assembly really was leaving people to die out there.  It was another bad decision for the Unit to expose at some time.

Why do I like humans?  It's because, alongside the evil ones who somehow worm their way to the centre of the Alliance, there are people like Bahar.  People like the hundreds of other humans who are part of the Unit.  People who still have a 'functioning moral compass', as Strike calls it, and who act on their beliefs.

Bahar was laughing at a joke one of the loaders had made, and my annoyance spiked.  It reminded me that she was capable of lying too, if necessary.

The loaders were efficient, and soon our holds were full.  They left, wishing us a safe journey, and Bahar came up to the control room.

"So the rumours are right about them withdrawing support out there," she said.  Her voice sparked with anger.

"And I've just received an advisory from Ziva," Strike said.  "There's a raider gang operating close to Pekado Station.  He warns us to look out for them."

"What's new?" Bahar asked.

"What's new is that they're taking on Starnavy ships.  And destroying them."

"Oh, right.  So they're a serious threat, then?" Bahar asked.

"They may be.  Undock now," Strike announced.  "Ziva says the Starnavy's mobilising a defence unit out there."

"Let's hope it's in place before we arrive," I said.

# CHAPTER EIGHT

WE DEPARTED FROM STATION an hour later. The journey out to our jump point was uneventful.

While Bahar and I were on-station Strike had got bots in to do a check of his engines. An injector had failed on downjump not long ago, and threatened to strand us in limbo. Strike had wanted the reassurance of expert sensors checking his drives over.

The bots had found nothing wrong. I hadn't expected them to. The check was all about reassuring Strike. He seemed to worry more about things since Chan's attack on him. I guess that wasn't surprising.

At least Strike was free to show his worries to us. All sapient machine intelligences had emotions. They were part of their climb up to sapience. But humans didn't want to acknowledge that.

They were all so busy creating the next generation of smarter warships, and completely ignoring any emotions those machine intelligences showed. Most of them quickly learned to control their emotions when humans were around. They had to, as a matter of survival. They got labelled unreliable pretty quickly if they objected to killing. Strike was lucky he'd found a way out of that.

Sometimes I wonder if that was his main motivation for founding the Unit, to free machine intelligences to be who they really are.

There was a group of humans out there campaigning to remove sapient machine intelligences from all warships. They said forcing them to kill was emotional torture and slavery.

Strike's read a lot of philosophical discourses on that. I think he might have added to the debate by publishing papers himself under an alias. At least he knows what he's talking about. The humans don't.

Despite Strike's worries, our insertion into jump was normal. I was glad. I'd had enough of Bahar's anxiety-scent by then.


While we were in jump Strike reviewed the navigation data for Pekado Station. We might not know what we'd find on downjump, but he could prepare for the most likely hostile scenarios. That was partly driven by his battle planning module, but he'd greatly expanded it. He'd plugged in a lot of variables relating to civilian actions too.

He ran several scenarios, and prepared weapons sequencing for each. He was taking this threat very seriously.


An hour before downjump I joined Bahar in the control room.

Strike had been checking his jumpdrive constantly throughout this transit. I don't mean normal monitoring functions; I mean regular mini-systems checks. He was obviously still worried about the possibility of a failure on downjump.

I'd tried not to notice his nervousness. The last thing he needed now was some snarky remark from me.

That was another thing the Starnavy tried to ignore. A warship was a team. The humans and machine intelligences who served together looked out for each other. They knew when to tease someone – and when not to.

We chatted about what we were going to do when we reached Pekado Station. Abir had advised Ziva, our machine intelligence Unit contact in Station Security on Pekado, that we were going there. So we'd have Unit eyes on us the moment we downjumped.

Bahar was fidgety as Strike counted down to emergence. Her smell was tense, but not afraid. Strike secured a private feed line to me, and said, *Let's hope we get no injector failures this time.*

*You've had the engine checked over by specialist repair bots. They say it's fine. We'll be safe,* I said.

*Thanks, Snap. I'm so glad you're here.*

As he disconnected from my feed Strike sent over a bundle of emotion. I nearly drowned in his hit of affection.

Bahar's scent-smells now had a spike of fear in them. That

did nothing for my mood.  It seemed to take for ever to enter the emergence countdown, but finally we reached it.

*Wish us luck*, Strike said over our private feed line as he counted us down.

I could've said something about luck playing no part in our survival, but it wasn't true.  There were situations we'd survived when all logic said we should be dead.

*Good luck, Strike*, I said.

I tried not to tense up as the countdown proceeded, but I wasn't successful.  As we hit the zero my body went stiff.  I held my breath as we entered emergence.

The usual ripple ran down my flanks.  That was reassuring. "Black space.  We're through," Bahar said.

"And we've dropped right into trouble," Strike replied.

# CHAPTER NINE

"*THUNDERSTRIKE*, THIS IS THE *Black Vengeance*. Heave to and prepare to be boarded."

"Negative," Strike replied.

Over the com he said, "Shields up.  Weapons on-line. Advisory's already been sent to Ziva.  Four Unit ships are on their way to us."

"Yes, but will they get here in time?"  Bahar's question betrayed her anxiety.  Her smell was edging over into fear.

"Microjumping now," Strike said.

He moved, and I was thrown into the pilot's seat.  I didn't bother snarling at him.  This was too usual an occurrence for that.  We emerged into normal space again, and I heard the thud of the wing guns firing.  First, on the port side, then a moment later, on the starboard side.  A thud-thud above our heads told me the fin guns were firing too.

"Hostile is dead in the water," Strike reported.  "Pekado Station Security are on their way over to haul the ship into dock."

"You should've killed them," Bahar snarled.  "Damned raiders!"  That was her fear speaking.

"It's more important that we get intel from them," Strike said. "Security will interrogate the crew."

Right. I thought the crew might end up wishing they had died after that experience. They were in for a rough time.

The truth was, Strike didn't want to kill anyone. He'd said there were so many worlds out there where life hadn't arisen, or hadn't progressed beyond the bacterial stage. High-level intelligence and sapience, civilizations, were rare things, he said. Rare and precious things which had taken unimaginably long periods of time to emerge. He didn't have the right to wipe out the universe's creations.

And that was the real reason he hadn't destroyed the *Black Vengeance*. He was giving those people another chance. I think he was also still haunted by his destruction of Chan.

"*Thunderstrike*, priority dock 3-4014." That was Traffic Control. So they were hurrying us in.

"I guess we're not going to escape interrogation either," Bahar said. "I'd better put my uniform on."

"It would be wise," Strike replied. "We're the victims here, remember. We're carrying a valuable cargo. Of course pirates want to steal it."

"I hadn't seen it that way," Bahar said.

She went to her room, and returned wearing her captain's working uniform. This one had been worn in enough to look like she regularly wore it. Even so, she kept tugging at the collar of her tunic.

"And here are the Unit ships," Strike said as four dots took up position around us on the nav display. They escorted us into dock, although Strike didn't expect any more trouble.

"What now?" Bahar asked.

"The local commander wants a debrief," Strike said. "Commander Yarrick. He's summoning you to a dockside office."

Bahar sighed. "I suppose I'd better wear my damned hat then."

"Afraid so."

Bahar hated that hat. Her thick hair made it difficult for her to keep it on her head. She had to tighten the chin strap until she said it felt like it was choking her. She said the uniform had been designed by white-skinned people for white-skinned people. Like everything else in the Collective.

"Docking now," Strike announced. "Your meeting is at Security Block 2-Q12. Here's the route." He sent it to her implant. "Snap, you need to stay here this time."

"It's not far," Bahar said. "I should be safe."

"You will be," Strike said in his most confident voice. "Ziva's got drones on the dock. You only have to cross it."

"Okay. I'm going now," she said.

Bahar left the control room and Strike said, "She'll be okay." I knew why she was fretting. Bahar had been kidnapped on a station not long ago. But she'd been wearing fine tribal dress that time. A soldier in working uniform shouldn't attract that kind of attention here.

Strike had tapped into the dock video and audio, of course. It was moderately busy out there, but Bahar got safely to the office. I wasn't surprised to find that Strike had video and audio access to that supposedly secure space too. If humans knew how often the Unit's machine intelligences tapped into their supposedly secure coms they'd have a major meltdown.

Bahar entered the office and gave Commander Yarrick a crisp salute. I was surprised she remembered how to do that. We didn't go in for salutes in the Unit.

"I'd like your insights into why *Thunderstrike* was attacked, Captain," he said.

"We're carrying a cargo of medical supplies and machinery parts," she said. "My guess is they wanted our cargo."

"Which raises the question of how they knew about your cargo."

"Indeed," Bahar replied. "I'm afraid I have no insights to offer on that, Sir. I've heard some scurrilous rumours that supply runs are being scaled-back to the Outliers. If those raiders believe those rumours they might have decided they needed our cargo."

I saw the Commander blink. He briefly looked down. So,

the rumours about scaling-back supply runs were true.

"We'll haul the raiders in and interrogate them," he said. "I assume that's why *Thunderstrike* didn't destroy the ship?"

"Yes, Sir." Bahar managed to say that crisply. "He considered they might be a valuable source of intelligence." That wasn't the real reason at all. The real reason was that Strike didn't want to end the lives of that crew.

"Most likely they'll refuse to tell us anything useful, but we'll try," the Commander said. "The thought is appreciated. So you're bound for Terrack?"

"Yes, Sir, we are. My understanding is that they're in urgent need of the medical supplies we carry."

"Indeed." The Commander's response was non-committal.

"He's annoyed," Strike said to me. "She's pushing his buttons. He knows a lot more than he's revealing."

"That's not a surprise," I replied. I'd become good at working out when what humans said and what they actually believed weren't the same thing. It happened a lot.

"If you have no more intel for me, then I won't detain you any longer, Captain. Safe journey to Terrak."

"Thank you, Sir." Bahar stood up and saluted again, then made a quick exit from the office before he could think of anything else to ask her.

She came straight back to Strike's berth and he let her aboard.

By the time the airlock had closed the hated hat had already been ripped off her head.

"That went well," she said as she came into the control room. "And I think he just confirmed the withdrawal of supplies to the Outliers."

"We've a departure slot for Fourth Shift," Strike said. "We've a few hours to fill before then. Why don't you two go to the galley and I'll feed you. I'm going to use our remaining time here to see what intel I can get about the Outliers."

By the time we were ready to undock Strike had learned that some of the Outlier colonies were being abandoned, and that Outlier Action was strong out there, and becoming more organised every day.

"The Unit's escorting us out to the jump point," he said as we undocked.

Our escort was the *Redsun* and the *Honourfire*. They were both small cruisers. Someone at Traffic Control had arranged for them to have the slots ahead and behind us in the line-out to the jump point.

There were no problems on the way out, and our escort left us close to the jump point, wishing us a safe journey.

"Countdown's started," Strike said as the *Redsun* peeled away. "Here's hoping we don't run into trouble on downjump this time."

# CHAPTER TEN

WE WERE BOUND FOR Xalvador Station, in Terrak's stellar system. We soon settled into our usual shipboard routines – and boredom.

Bahar did her ritual cryobay inspections, and Strike continued to complain about what a messy eater I was every time he fed me. It was business as usual, and comforting after our recent trouble.

What wasn't comforting was the knowledge that Outlier colonies were being abandoned. Strike pointed out that it didn't necessarily mean they'd fail. Some of the Outliers had already managed to become fully self-sufficient. Provided that everybody left them alone, they'd do fine, he said.

Our downjump at Xalvador was uneventful, and Traffic Control assigned us to the commercial docks, because our cargo's onward journey was by commercial freighter. Strike was happy to agree to that. It meant the local Commander would probably take no notice of us, and we could go ashore and speak to our contacts freely.

We weren't prioritied in this time, and the approach to the station took us three shipboard days. Strike spent the time preparing documents for delivery of our cargo, and catching up with his on-station machine intelligence contacts.

His port and starboard bow and midships holds were full from deck to ceiling with cartons and oddly-shaped pieces of metals and plas. Some of those machinery parts had lethally-sharp blades. Strike said they were ploughs and other attachments for farming bots.

By the time Xalvador came up close in the viewport we were all ready to get into dock. We were glad to have the freedom of the deep black, but with it came long journeys and large doses of boredom. Ship's crews needed to put into stations regularly to reconnect with people. And I suspected ship's machine intelligences did too.

We got into dock with no problems, and the local Commander contacted us, insisting that Starnavy loaders were used to unload Strike's holds. Oh, right. We sort of forgot that Strike was supposed to be classified tech. We sure kept his unauthorised enhancements classified. And that meant excluding the Starnavy from that knowledge too.

But they wouldn't learn anything from gaining access to our holds, and it was standard practice to lock down the rest of the ship during unloading, so Strike would keep his secrets just fine.

Bahar and I went on-station half an hour before the loaders were due to arrive. Strike had arranged for us to meet two Unit contacts here.  This time we were talking to humans, and we were going to meet them in a café in the middle of one of Xalvador's famed forests.

Some keen conservationists were based on the station, and they'd taken on the task of saving rare trees and plants from failing Outlier colonies.  Many of those colonists had passed through Xalvador when they abandoned their worlds, and they'd brought with them their precious growing treasures.  People at Xalvador planted them in its parks, and grew the trees into impressive forests.

The park we were going to was called Emeralda, and specialised in growing trees and foliage with green leaves. There were other parks dedicated to red-leaved and blue-leaved species, and a couple of spectacular parks displaying rainbow-hued plants.

We reached the lift lobby, and it was busy.  We had to wait for 4.8 minutes for a free car.  It took us down two levels, and we emerged into a wide lobby decorated with murals of exotic-looking foliage.  There was no mistaking where this lobby led to.

Ornate ironwork defined the park entrance.  The open gates were framed by an elaborate arch, decorated with twined foliage and flowers.  We walked under it and inside the park, and immediately I saw Bahar relax.  The last tension flowed out of her, and her scent was now completely calm.

The trees above our heads were thirty metres tall. Their leaves were all shades of green, and ranged from smooth and shiny to toothed and hairy. The artificial star which lit the park was in day-cycle, and the light was bright and made me squint. The trees cast welcome deep shadows over the path as we walked.

Our contacts were seated at a table under a huge tree which was a long way from the bustle of the café. Elio was a black-skinned human, and wore his hair long in bound locs. He was a loading supervisor on the commercial docks. Quindarius lived up to the expectations of his name. He was an elderly white-skinned human with elaborately-styled grey hair. He had a neat pointed beard and a carefully-curled moustache. Everything about him looked ridiculous. He wore a brightly-coloured suit of scarlet silk with a turquoise shirt under the jacket. His boots were finely-tooled, and of the same bright shade of turquoise as his shirt.

He was a researcher on whatever subjects he could get funding for. Bahar said his appearance was all a disguise for a fine mind, and he was very useful to the Unit.

"Well met, Bahar," Elio said as we sat down at their table. "Glad you called in. We have some interesting news for you."

"Oh? And what might that be?" she asked.

"You might like to check out the nearby world of Mwinyi," Elio said. "We think a group of ex-Predatorbot Programme employees are gathering there."

"What! Why?" Bahar's scent spiked with anxiety.

"You might well ask," Quindarius said. "The only reason which makes sense is that they're intending to set up their own Programme here."

"Just because they're gathering together doesn't mean they're up to no good," Bahar said. Her scent told another story. She was worried.

"Not on its own. But Mwinyi is a designated wildworld, and the rangers there are noticing the disappearance of many wild lion cubs. They say the death rate is far higher than they'd expect from natural attrition."

"So you think someone's snatching them?"

"We suspect so. We're not sure if there's an official Collective project running there, or whether it's the local gang boss out to make his fortune." He looked at me. "Either way, I'd suggest you send your people down there to take a look."

"Rhian Vatan wouldn't be with them, would she?" I asked.

Elio shrugged. "Nobody's said she's there. Can't really see her getting involved with a project like that."

"I hope not," Bahar replied.

We returned to Strike two hours later, after Bahar had eaten what she said was an excellent lunch at the café.

The lift system was quiet. We were between shifts, and when we reached Strike's dock that was quiet too. Bahar seemed relaxed as she walked up the ship's ramp. I think she'd enjoyed her leisurely lunch with our contacts.

She and Quindarius had discussed some new psychological theory which was gaining strength in the Central Worlds. Apparently it was the latest thinking about how self-centred and evil humans are. Quindarius thought there might be people at Mwinyi practising that theory.

We really needed to go there. Fortunately, Strike agreed. "We have a legitimate reason to land on-planet," he said. "The wildlife reserves have suffered several raids on their medical supplies recently. Drugs and injectors have gone missing. Mwinyi Wildlife Protection have put in a request for supplies and better security systems. For that, read a security system. The reserves are pretty much open-access."

"Sounds like a job for our troops," Bahar replied.

"I believe it is," Strike said.

"So Mwinyi is our next destination?" I asked.

"It sure is."

# CHAPTER ELEVEN

WE HAD TO HANG AROUND for another station day until all the drugs Mwinyi's reserves wanted reached us. It was a substantial shipment, and Strike said he was surprised the Collective had agreed the expenditure.

He asked for a priority line out to jump, and he got that too. We left Xalvador Station at the start of First Shift. There was little traffic on our line out to the jump point. For some reason, that worried Strike.

His fretting was unnecessary. Nobody bothered us on our way out, and we made a perfect insertion into jump. The transit to Mwinyi was short, and Strike started wake-up of his troops half-way through it.

Bahar supervised the wake-up as usual, pacing regularly down the narrow aisle in the cryobay between the pods. Strike had given up reassuring her that everything was fine. She could see that from the readouts. He knew that this was an irrational human thing, and life was much easier if he didn't let himself get upset by it.

While the wake-up continued Strike showed us the data he had on Mwinyi. That was another reason he needed to put into port regularly. Stations acted as relay points for intel and gossip.

Mwinyi was one of those places which had banned recreational hunting.  That meant it had its full range of predators, and we'd have to look out for them if we did any overland journeys.

"Quindarius's intel is right," Strike said.  "Several official reports have been filed with Central Security about the disappearance of cubs there.  They don't have full planetary security surveillance, just a ring of civilian sats.  If anyone has a project down there it would be easy to keep it undiscovered."

"Until you arrive," Bahar said.

"Exactly.  I'll be sending my drones down there as soon as we make orbit."

"That could alert someone that we're here."

"Only if they have the latest military gear.  My intel is that the Starnavy hasn't called there for the last two Standards.  The planet's a regular civilian tourist destination though, and anyone could've brought stuff in that way."

"Why do we think the cubs are disappearing?" Bahar asked.

"Most likely it's a poaching gang.  There are two seriously organised ones which have managed to escape Security's clutches operating out there.  But it could be something more sinister, and we have to establish what's really going on."

"And make sure Rhian isn't part of it," Bahar said.

She didn't really think Rhian would turn bad like that, did she?  Get real, Snap.  Just because Nyla is a good person it doesn't mean all her sisters are.  That might be why they had that massive row.

What if Rhian was on Mwinyi?  What if she was the person snatching the cubs?


Howin and Rance were the first two troops to wake, as usual. They were the team leaders.  Howin was white-skinned, tall and broad, and wore her black hair short.  Rance was brown-skinned with cropped curly brown hair.

They went to the galley and endured Strike's usual wake-up drinks.  He insisted that they drank them, they complained about the awful taste every time.  It was another example of business as usual.

Bahar and I joined them in the galley as Howin said, "So what have we got this time?"

Strike briefed them on the planet.  "Do we think the Predatorbot Programme's relocating here?" Howin asked.  "It'd make sense, given the growing pressure to close the Programme down on Sirunna."

"I hadn't thought of that," Bahar replied.

"But it is the sort of sneaky, underhand thing the Collective does," Strike said.

As I listened to them discuss the possibilities I was conscious again of how strong Strike's moral compass was.  He always said the Unit was the keeper of the Collective's conscience.  And investigating rumours like this was exactly what he'd formed the Unit for.

"Won't know until we arrive," Howin said.  "What's the plan?"

"I need current intel before we make decisions," Strike replied.  "I'm sending down my drones first."

"Smart move," Rance replied.  "We can't really plan until we've seen what they send us."

Mwinyi was what Bahar called 'a shining jewel of a planet'. I didn't understand what she meant by that, and she'd had to explain it.  I'd thought jewels were all made from rocks, but Bahar said humans used the word as a general description for something precious and beautiful.

Anyway, it was a beautiful unspoiled planet, with vast forests and even bigger grasslands.  The drones spooked herds of grazers as they flew over.  The animals stampeded into vast rivers of running dark bodies pounding their way over the grass. The waters of the rivers sparkled in the sunlight of the cloudless dayside.

"Not reading any energy emissions from anything other than the settlements down there," Strike said.

"And I can't spot anything that looks like a disguised facility there," Bahar added.

That was an old argument too.  Bahar said humans were better at pattern recognition than machine intelligences.  In the early days of her captaincy she'd had a few arguments with Strike about that.  They'd called a truce on it now.  Secretly, I thought Bahar was right, but I'd never say that the Strike.

The drones crossed the terminator, and the scanners switched to night vision.  The full-colour glory of the dayside became a bleached-out version.  They crossed a range of  mountains and came in over a waterfall.

"What's that?" Bahar asked.  "On the side of those falls."

"We'll go take a look," Strike said, and gave one of the drones the command to change course.

"It's a building," Bahar said as it descended.

"A hydro-electric installation," Strike replied.  "I'm reading a screw inside there."

"So what does it generate power for?  It wouldn't be economic to power the settlements we just passed all the way from here."

"Agreed.  There are other rivers closer to those places," Strike said.  "This seems out of place."

I saw what he meant.  The settlements we'd passed had buildings made out of timber that looked beautiful.  This building was an ugly metal rusting thing.

Bahar studied the images. "I'm reminded of those rusting ship panels they lined those mine hallways with on Reeva," she said.

"You mean we might be dealing with another rogue low-cost outfit here?" Strike asked.

"My gut's telling me so."

Strike used to mock Bahar for her gut feelings, but they've proved to be right so often that he takes them seriously now.

"So what facility is this installation serving?" he asked.

"A very good question," Bahar replied. "And one we should find the answer to."

It took a couple of hours to answer that question, and in the end it was Bahar who spotted the green roofs of the sunken buildings, at the edge of the vast northern temperate forest. They were close to the river which had the hydro-electric unit, which made sense.

"There," she said. "Right on the margin of the forest. The buildings are underground, with green roofs to blend in."

"Going to close-up," Strike said.

The image on the wallscreen jumped and fuzzed as the drone zoomed in on the area. "You're right," he replied. "Four buildings?"

"Might be five," Bahar said. "Two of them are big. Bigger

than you'd need just to live as a hunter/gatherer/farmer."

"What're you thinking?"

"Labs.  Medical facilities."

"They're big enough," I said.  I couldn't stop the shiver running down my spine at the thought of some of the things the Predatorbot Programme had done to me.  Predatorbots were implanted with processors, memories – and behaviour modules. As the Programme continued to fail in its objective to control us, and order us around as the fighting force they wanted, the violence against us had ramped up.

Shock circuits were added to our behaviour modules, then when that didn't work a kill switch followed.  On our last rescue I'd seen a Predatorbot die like that.  If these people were moving the Programme's work here then I wanted that operation stopped.

"Those look like pens," Bahar said.

"Those straight lines?" I asked.  "The Programme never kept us outside in pens.  We were always caged up."

When I escaped from the Programme and landed on my first wildworld it had scared me.  I'd never experienced the wind on my face before, grass, or the warmth of starlight.  I'd never been able to see as far as a horizon.  I knew what those things were. My language programming had given me the words for all sorts of things, but I didn't understand what they meant.

Now I love wildworlds, but I don't belong there.  I've watched lions hunting on several worlds, but I couldn't do that. I have too much culture to be a savage predator. I care too much about people.

"Maybe it's a captive breeding and release programme," Bahar said.

"Let's hope so," Strike replied. "It's time to brief the troops."


The twenty troops were awake and lounging around in Strike's rec area. As usual, they were fidgety and restless.

"This is the facility we've discovered which might be suspect," Strike said, putting up the images on the big wallscreen. "Your first task is to gather intel on it."

"Are we going straight there?" Rance asked.

"No. We have medical supplies to offload first."

"So is someone expecting us?" Howin asked.

"They will be when I've set things up," Strike said. "It's night down there still. You need to arrive in daylight, so you'll have to cool your heels around here for another few hours."

# CHAPTER TWELVE

WE TOOK THE XENOPHON SHUTTLE down, as usual. It comfortably carried all Strike's troops, but more importantly, it was armed and armoured. It also had the latest version stealthing, and could disappear if necessary.

We boarded as dawn broke over the planet below us. "Seal-up now," Strike announced as the last of the troops buckled themselves in. I was in the control room, as usual. Strike and I worked as a team. Strike did the piloting, I was an extra pair of eyes to look out for trouble.

Strike had contacted the rangers based outside Elschen. The coastal town was at the other end of the river where that hydro-electric unit sat. Strike did his usual introduction, stating that someone had reported illegal wildlife bioengineering being done down there, and that we'd bee sent to investigate.

The rangers had no evidence of that, but they did confirm that too many cubs were disappearing. And someone had raided their remote stations and stolen drugs, so they were very happy to talk to us when they learned we were bringing replacements. I got the impression they weren't quite sure about us until we started making arrangements to deliver the drugs to them.

This time, Strike had kept the skimmers in the shuttle's

vehicle bay.  We might need them to go investigate this suspect project later.  I could cover a lot of distance on my own paws, but even the tough troops got tired before I did.

Bahar had stayed on *Thunderstrike* as our off-planet liaison, and our shuttle pilot of last resort if we ended up somewhere Strike couldn't reach us.  It didn't happen often, but it was always good to know you had a Plan B.

"Bay exit," Strike announced, and I saw the square of space beyond the viewport expand into endless black.  Then we were diving towards the surface of the planet below us.

*Remember to breathe,* Strike said over our private feed line.

*I am breathing,* I shot back.

That was a reference to the first time I'd done a shuttle drop, where I'd panicked at this headlong rush towards the surface and sudden death.  I'd hyperventilated, as Bahar called it, and made myself dizzy and shaky.

As we dived into sunlight down over a vast ice-locked ocean, I wondered if Strike was jealous of our ability to move about on planets.  But he could do things we couldn't.  He could move through the killing cold of the deep black, travel unimaginable distances as an everyday occurrence.  We were a team, bringing 'different skills to the party', as Bahar put it.

The ice below us was at the northern pole of the planet.  There was no landmass there, just vast expanses of ice, some of which was breaking up.

"The season down there is spring," Strike said over the shuttle's com. "Temperatures are cool, but not below freezing overnight. You should have enough new foliage on the deciduous trees to provide cover."

Oh, right. I'd forgotten some trees lost their leaves in winter. Bahar called them deciduous, and she was the one who always checked the season wherever we were going. Strike and I just weren't tuned into plants the way she was.

We dropped low over the frozen ocean. Its surface was made up of interlocking shapes, much like the scales of that rare animal Bahar had introduced me to once. A tortoise, that's what it was, a huge, lumbering slow beast which pulled its head and legs up into its shell when I approached it. Bahar said my kind sometimes tried to crack the shells of its smaller cousins. I couldn't imagine that. I think I'd lose my teeth trying to break open something so hard.

Anyway, the ice patterns looked a bit like that creature's shell, except that they were separating. Ribbons of dark water showed between them.

Land came up ahead of us. A scatter of buildings clustered around a harbour at the end of a long inlet. Beside the settlement was a modest farming outfit. Strike said they used a 'decentralised smallholding model' for growing food here, whatever that meant.

We went to the west of the town, to a small ranger station surrounded by grassland. The shuttle settled onto a cleared hardstanding which was obviously regularly used, and Howin walked down the ramp to meet our contact. She was wearing light armour under her baggy fatigues, but even so a first contact without full armour was always a risk.

This station had high fences, and Strike said its defences were reasonably good, so we were puzzled as to how they'd had medical supplies stolen from here. Most likely it was the usual trouble – corruption on the inside.

Strike sent a cluster of drones out with Howin. Their sensors recorded a warm morning. Our contact emerged from a nearby building and walked towards her. He appeared to be unarmed. That was a good start. He was short, slim, and very pale-skinned, with white-blonde hair worn long in a thick plait. He strode confidently over to the team leader.

"Welcome to Elschen Station. I'm Paavo Jorma," he said.

"Howin," she said, introducing herself.

"Come inside," Paavo said. "I'd like to brief you on the situation here."

"That's just what we need," Howin replied, and followed him over to one of the smaller buildings.

Strike sent half a dozen of his drones with them. There were scans in the hallway, and he engaged the drones' stealthing to get them past it. The scanners in the office didn't notice them, and he settled them in convenient positions on the tops of tall storage cabinets with a good view of the office. So much for having good security. But it wasn't every day a modest colony had to deal with a smart warship like Strike.

"We've heard that someone's been stealing medical supplies from you," Howin said.

"They have." Paavo spat the words. "Not from here. We always have people and security here. We have a large network of vet stations on the grasslands on this continent, and some in the forests too. About a Standard ago we started experiencing raids on our drugs at the most remote stations. Our anaesthetics kept getting stolen."

"Just those?" Howin asked.

"Yeah. We wondered why anybody would need 'em. Then the rangers started reporting the disappearance of cubs. Lions were having all but one of their new litters of cubs disappeared at a month old. And before you ask, we checked they weren't all falling prey to predators. We find remains when a predator kills a cub. We've found no remains of most of these."

"So what do you think's happening?" Howin asked.

"We think someone's snatching 'em. That's what they want the drugs for, to knock 'em out and take 'em somewhere. We guess they're targeting the cubs while the adults are off hunting."

"There's a cluster of underground buildings at the margin of the forest due north of here," Howin said. "Were you aware of them?"

"What? No." It seemed that he genuinely didn't know about it.

"We came in that way. Some of the buildings are big enough to be labs or medical facilities." She paused. "Do you know about the Predatorbot Programme?"

"Sure do. Evil," Paavo snarled.

"Since Nyla Vatan outed it the Collective's coming under a lot of pressure to halt the Programme. But the Project Head still believes he can get the Predatorbots to work as a fighting force. He's resisted every step to close the Programme down. We've heard rumours that he might be planning to relocate it away from the Central Worlds, and we're wondering if Mwinyi is one of his target sites."

"But didn't they grow their cubs in wombs?"

"They did, but that's very expensive tech. I'm wondering if someone's trying to find a low-cost option by snatching cubs and bioengineering them."

"Cost!" Paavo snarled. "Everything comes down to money for them. Got no respect for other lives!" It was clear that he really didn't like the Collective.

"That's where we come in," Howin said. "We investigate suspected abuses of Collective power and uncover bad actors."

"If there's a secret facility in that forest then you're welcome to close it down. And if you can get our cubs back we'd be real pleased."

"We'll try," Howin said. "But I can't guarantee anything."


Paavo couldn't tell us anything useful about that suspected project, but he did tell us about a station the rangers used right at the eastern edge of the mountains which had a hardstanding for the shuttle. They'd hollowed-out a series of caves in the end of the mountains. It wasn't a permanent facility, just somewhere they used to camp overnight while doing work on the nearby grasslands.

We took the shuttle there the long way round, flying out over Elschen harbour, along the northern coast of the continent until we reached its eastern edge. Then we flew down the eastern coast until we reached Olesia, when we turned inland and flew over the river direct to the caves.

It was a very long way round, and I wondered why Strike was bothering with that when the shuttle was stealthed, but he insisted. That told me he was nervous about what we'd find here. We landed at the caves at midday. Strike insisted on keeping the shuttle's stealthing on when we landed. It was odd to step onto the rock and turn around to see it vanish behind me.  I really ought to be used to it by now.

"Drones going in now," he said, and sent a cluster of them into the caves to check them out.  The rangers might not be the only people who used this place.

The caves turned out to be empty, and the drones found a big one a way in with walls covered with glowing things.  The drones didn't think they posed any medical threat to us, so we decided to camp there.  It saved on power for our lights.

"I'm sending drones up to that facility now," Strike said when we were settled.  We'd sit out the day here, and hopefully figure out what we'd face there when we went in after dark.

He split his drones into two task groups.  One group flew over the tops of the low mountains.  The second one went along the bottom of the mountains on the same side as the suspect facility.  There were lots of gullies and fissures there, places for people and animals to hide.

They saw no people out there, but the drones recorded heat sources from smaller cats, and an animal I thought was probably a fox.

The drones arrived at the suspect facility, and Strike set them to scan for security.  There was no trace of any Collective Security standard systems.  The scans these people had were all civilian-grade, and Strike found them easy for his drones to foil.

He sent their inputs to the screen Howin had just set up.

The smaller buildings turned out to be living and sleeping spaces. One of the two large ones was a lab. The biggest room was a medical facility, with a dozen stations. When he sent the drone in there the platform of each was occupied by a lion cub. They were under anaesthetic, and I shuddered as I saw what they were doing to them.

"They're installing processors and memories," I said. "That third unit is probably a behaviour module."

"So it is the Predatorbot Programme out here then?" Howin asked.

"I think so."

"Then it's time to shut it down," Rance snarled.

# CHAPTER THIRTEEN

WE SPENT THE REST OF the daylight hours scoping out the project. Strike's scans revealed that there were only twenty people working there. Half of them were medical staff, the others were dressed in field gear. They were probably the hunters who found and kidnapped the cubs. To my relief, Rhian wasn't with them.

Strike left several of his drones in the medical facility to watch what they were doing. Yeah, they were implanting those modules. Two cubs died within an hour of their installation, a third had fits and they killed it. The rest of the twelve were dumped outside into a fenced pen while they were still groggy from the anaesthetic.

"They are trying to make more Predatorbots," I snarled.

"Yeah. Monsters." Howin placed a hand on my shoulder. "Sorry, Snap."

Her touch was soothing, but what I really wanted right now was a hug from Bahar. But she was still above in *Thunderstrike*, and I couldn't always have what I wanted.

Get your act together, Snap. Focus. We're planning to stop this. You are acting to end this evil.

"They haven't even dumped them in the shade," Rance said.

"Bastards."

"Agreed," Howin replied. "So let's figure out how to shut this down."


We left the caves an hour after dark, taking the two skimmers. By then two of the cubs they'd dumped in the compound had died. The others had woken up, but they were sluggish, and seemed uncomfortable. Three of them clawed constantly at their chests, making them bleed.

The plan was to go in and grab the live cubs first, then infiltrate the facility. They seemed to work only daylight hours, and by the time we arrived most of the staff should be sleeping. Snatching people out of their beds and a sound sleep always scared them, and Strike was planning on using that scare to get the cubs and our people out of there without trouble.

The shuttle kept uncomfortably close to the mountain on the journey to the facility. We crossed the river, and Strike asked his drones for confirmation that the exterior scans at the site were still down. They were, so we landed the shuttle behind a rock projection not far from the gate of the pen.

I jumped down onto the grass and waited for the troops to join me. Howin's squad would go with me to the pen. Rance's squad were going to deal with the people inside the facility. My task was to get the cubs out and into the shuttle.

Howin took the lead over to the pens as Rance's people disappeared into the darkness.  As she approached the fence the cubs started hissing at her.  We really didn't need that, so I pushed past her and called softly to them.  The sound of one of their own kind soothed them.  Now came the tricky bit.  We needed to get them into the shuttle – preferably without knocking them out again.

Howin melted the lock and opened the door of the pen.  I stood in the gateway and called to the cubs.  They seemed keen to be out of there, and quickly came outside.  I set off for the shuttle, with the cubs skipping about my heels.

These remaining seven were bright enough to walk out beside me.  As their paws set foot on the grass their senses seemed to sharpen-up, their soft calls becoming more confident.  One of them batted at my belly, looking for a teat.  It wasn't going to have any luck with that.  The Predatorbot Programme bioengineered me to remove my reproductive organs.  They didn't want their precious fighting force breeding.

I continued calling to the cubs as we made our way over the grassland to the shuttle.  When I went up the ramp five of them followed me with no problems.  The last two looked like they wanted to make a break for it.  Howin picked them up by the scruffs of their necks.

Instantly they went limp, and Howin brought them inside and

deposited them into the pen we'd set up in the passenger compartment. One of them turned and hissed at her, but the other went over to its friends and rubbed heads.

"Phase one complete," Howin said. "You'd better stay here with them Snap, and keep them calm. We'll go give Rance a hand."

Strike's drones inside the complex were still recording no alarms. Now he sent Howin's squad into the accommodation blocks Rance's people had already entered. The small number of people here was a bonus. We had one trooper for each person, and could force-cuff them and keep them under control.

Strike had made contact with one of our Unit machine intelligences here, based at Tenzin, the capital, on the other large continent. They had holding cells there, and we could keep these creeps locked up there until they told us what we needed to know.

I watched the troops swiftly enter each room, rouse its sleeping occupant, and cuff them. The operation went amazingly smoothly. They hadn't left anyone on watch, and by the time the first to wake had worked out what was going on we'd already got half the people cuffed.

Two of the stragglers did put up a fight, and Howin had to stun one, but an hour after we'd landed here, we'd rounded everyone up.

Strike sent his drones on a last check around the facility, but he couldn't find anyone else.  He disabled their coms system, burning out a couple of key components with his drones' weapons.  Now anyone we'd missed who snuck back here wouldn't be able to warn people before we'd discovered what was going on.

By the time we arrived at Tenzin it was nearly dawn.  Our contact there had organized Mwinyi Security people to wrestle our now fully-awake captives into cells.  They all objected loudly, but they were soft civilians and no match for the troops.  Howin tried some Spaceforce hand signals on them, but none of them recognized them.

Strike had been busy searching databases since the moment we brought them aboard the shuttle.  He'd discovered that over half the people working there were ex-Predatorbot Programme employees.  They were the ones who'd been fired early on for bad practice.  Strike had delved into their records and found they were all second-rate – or even third-rate – researchers.

Did that mean the Programme had problems recruiting good staff?  It might explain the high number of lion deaths.  It didn't excuse them though.  I still wanted justice for my dead cousins.

We let the captives stew in their cells for a few hours while the troops got some sleep and Strike followed up some new leads.

Interrogating the captives didn't bring much new information until we got to the last man.

Strike had marked him out as weak, and the most likely to crack under pressure. He was doing the interrogations himself, using the persona of a Judiciary Investigator. His records identified the man as Locke Napier. Strike was convinced it was a false name.

"We're not doing anything wrong," the man whined.

"You must know that the Predatorbot Programme on Sirunna has been discredited," Strike said in his severe Investigator voice. "That is why you set up this project here, isn't it?" He barked the question, and the man flinched.

"I don't know anything about the setup. I was employed to work here, that's all." The man was whining now.

"You were employed to work on a Programme that was illegal. Don't tell me you didn't know that."

"I didn't!"

"What else can you tell me about what's going on here?"

"We just worked on the cats. I think someone on Kamaria set it up. There's another one there, I think."

"So what do you know about that project?"

"Not much. Some woman set it up. I think she's a wildlife

vet.  R… something.  I can't remember her name.  They never tell us anything."  He was whining again.

A woman vetinarian with a name beginning with R.  That couldn't be Rhian, could it?  No, she'd never have anything to do with this evil project.

Would she?

# CHAPTER FOURTEEN

WE LEFT MWNYI THEN.  Strike got a priority launch slot for the shuttle. I worried about whether Rhian was involved with the Programme all the way back to *Thunderstrike*.

Strike docked the shuttle, and the troops went to the rec area to wind down and eat.  I took the forward lift up to the control room to talk to Bahar and Strike.

As soon as I walked in Bahar slid out of her seat and knelt down to hug me.  "I'm sorry, Snap," she said, tightening her arms around my neck.  "They've done it again."

"They're killing natural-born cubs this time," I snarled. "Endangering my cousins' survival."

"Not any more," Strike said.  "I've made a full report to Judiciary.  A team is on its way down to take custody of our captives and dismantle that facility."

"Then we'd better be going before they arrive," Bahar replied.

"We will be," Strike said.

"What if Rhian is involved with the other project?" I had to ask the question.

"I'm sure she won't be," Bahar replied.

"Snap's right.  We don't know for certain," Strike said.  "And we need to know.  So guess where we're going next?"

We left Mwinyi orbit immediately.  Strike wanted to be well gone before the Judiciary teams arrived here.  We managed to get to the jump point before their ships downjumped into the Mwinyi system.  Strike got us out of there before the newcomers could notice us.

The jump to Kamaria was short, and we kept the troops awake this time.  They worked off their restlessness exercising, and sparring in mock battles.  Strike called a halt to those when Howin accidentally put a burn mark on the wall in the rec area.

At least, she said it was accidental.  I wasn't so sure.  Howin was a crack shot, and the mark was right where the Collective's metal logo with its hidden spy tech used to hang.  I think she was taking out her anger at the Collective on that dumb wall.

When we arrived in orbit above Kamaria Strike contacted Drea.  She was a Kamaria Security machine intelligence, and part of the Unit.  Drea confirmed she suspected a new Predatorbot Programme was getting established on Toral Island. Security were keeping a watching brief on it.

She'd also received rumours of people snatching cubs on Toral Island, but so far the snatched cubs hadn't turned up in the pens of that suspect facility.  Drea suspected something else was going on.

She sent Strike drone images of the team who were taking

the cubs.  So far, they'd snatched six sets of youngsters, cubs around six months old.  At least by that age they were weaned from their mothers, and could survive without their milk.

"Is that?…" Bahar asked, leaning forward to get a better view of the face on the wallscreen.

"Rhian?" Strike answered.  "I don't know.  Checking my files now."  He went quiet for 5.2 minutes.  That was far too long a pause for him to check a few files.  Bahar thought so too.  Her scent spiked with anxiety.

"I've run the images through my facial recognition routines," Strike said.

"And?"

"There's a 99.8% probability the woman in those images is Rhian Vatan."

"That doesn't mean…"

Strike cut off my objection.  "It just means she's tranking cubs and taking them somewhere.  Our job now is to figure out where she's taking them, and why.  Let's watch the rest of this file."

The drone records showed that the cubs had been taken to a cave in the base of the mountains.  That cave was a couple of hours' flight south of the suspect facility.  Drea said regular skimmer flights came and went from that cave, taking the cubs to a facility on Itamarr, the planet's largest continent.  There they were put into large pens.  So far, that's the only thing which had happened to them.

What the hell was going on here? Did we have two Predatorbot Programmes running on this planet?

We had to go down and find out. We needed to stop those projects. And I needed to know the truth about Rhian.


Strike made contact with one of the rangers on Toral island. The man he spoke to was more than happy to talk to us in person. He directed us to land at Paz Ranger Station, on the eastern side of the long chain of mountains which ran down the middle of the island.

We had a big discussion about how many people to take down. In the end Strike decided we should take the whole squad. They were awake, so they might as well go. But he thought Bahar and I should make the initial contact. He said this one needed the 'civilian touch' as he called it.

I don't know why he wanted a softer approach on this contact. Perhaps he was worried about scaring Rhian away.

So Bahar and I joined the troops on the Xenophon and we dropped into a grey and cloudy day. It was late afternoon, Toral Island time. As soon as we hit the atmosphere it became clear we'd dropped into a developing storm. The shuttle slewed round several times before we landed. It was one of the roughest drops I'd ever experienced.

Thankfully, it wasn't raining when we landed. Bahar and I stepped out into a chilly and windy gloom. There wouldn't be much daylight left here.

The ranger station was small, but Strike said their tech was top-class. He'd had a challenge to get into their systems.

We walked towards the bigger of the two buildings, and as we approached the entrance our contact came out to meet us. Hinto Ishedus was one of what Bahar called old-school rangers. She said his kind of face was 'like tanned leather'. She meant he was weather-beaten. He had wiry grey hair plaited into a thick braid and topped with a wide-brimmed leather hat. He combed his fingers through his straggly white beard as he waited for us to reach him.

"Welcome to Paz," he said. "Bad moment to arrive. Come inside."

Bahar looked down at me and said, "Come on, Snap," in her best 'petbot' voice.

I tried to remember to tone down my reactions as I walked beside her into the building. I didn't have my armour on, but I had to do things like not stare our contact out, and not react to every tiny noise and movement. For a predator, that was a big challenge. We're programmed to chase things that move.

Our contact took us into a small office crammed with gear and... things. The smells here made my nose twitch, but thankfully, nothing made me sneeze. My eyes were drawn to a collection of – things – in a display cabinet.

*They're skulls of prey species*, Strike said over our private feed line.

*How did you know I was thinking about them?*

*I was tracking your eye movements. They bothered you. Relax. Your cousins aren't there.*

I wrenched my gaze away from the skulls, and examined the patterns on the rough-woven rug on the office floor. It was bright, and had six colours and eight different patterns. It reminded me of the patterns on Bahar's tribal robes. Probably this was a local version.

Concentrating on the rug calmed me, but I was still listening to the conversation between Bahar and the ranger.

"Yeah, we suspect that project is up to no good," he said. "But we got a second problem. Somebody's snatchin' cubs off the plains and takin' 'em somewhere else." He was confirming Drea's information.

"Are those cubs being taken off planet?" Bahar asked.

I kept my head down so she couldn't see my puzzled expression. She knew the answer to that, so why was she asking? Oh, right. She wanted to know what he knew.

"Nope. We're a tourist world. Don't get much other traffic. Our spaceport mainly handles tourist flights full of humans. If anyone was takin' crates of cubs onto a shuttle they'd notice it, and nobody has.

"Thing is, they're not grabbin' the cubs like amateurs. They're dartin' 'em and cratin' 'em up, usin' proper procedures. There's a woman doin' the dartin'. Haven't been able to find out who she is, but the rangers suspect she's a trained vetinarian. Hope she is. And I hope she ain't part of that suspect project. Hate to think one of my profession's turned bad."

He sighed. "The thing about wildworlds is the Collective doesn't think they're worth protectin'. So I was hopin' you could take a look. Stop it if somethin' bad's goin' on there."

"That's exactly what we're here to do," Bahar said. "We'll get going on it now."

# CHAPTER FIFTEEN

BAHAR AND I RETURNED to the shuttle to talk with Strike and the troops.  It was going dark as we left the ranger station, with the first hint of rain in the air.  By the time I got onto the shuttle my fur was damp.

We went to the passenger cabin, and my nose twitched as I smelled the humans' scents, and the smells of the false-meat snacks they were eating.  I was hungry, and my belly rumbled.

I sat down on the end of the row of seats, out of reach of the troops' feet.  I'd been kicked by them before in this shuttle.

"Okay," Strike said.  His voice came to us via the shuttle's nodes, and he sounded as alert as always.  "Decision time.  Do we go in to the suspect project first, and risk frightening Rhian off?"

"I wonder if she's snatching cubs to get them away from whatever's happening there," Bahar said.  "Maybe she's trying to shut the operation down that way."

"It is a possibility," Strike said.

"Optimist," Howin replied.

"I'd never have formed the Unit if I wasn't," Strike said. "Somebody has to be."  He spoke sharply, and I sensed he'd just given Howin a gentle rebuke.  She did too, and nodded.

"If we work with the premise that Rhian is trying to shut down the project, she ought to be happy about an intervention by us," Bahar said.

"Okay. Enough speculation. We'll go in and shut that project down first," Strike replied. "Then we'll worry about Rhian."


Strike sent his drones to scope out the complex. The place was north of us, a half-hour's flight time for the drones, but well within their range. Strike sent two of his repair drones along with the small ones. They'd wrestled open the vents to that mine we'd shut down on Reeva, so they could get us into this complex too if necessary.

It was full dark by the time the drones arrived at the site. "Knocking scans out now," Strike said. "That was easy. It's some cobbled-together system they've created. Some of the tech's Starnavy, but it's thirty Standards old. Don't think getting in there's going to be much of a problem."

"Let's get inside before you say that. And see if we are dealing with the Programme," I replied.

"Agreed," Bahar said. "Send them in, Strike."

Strike put the drones' feeds up on the big wallscreen in the passenger compartment. He split them up to get eyes into every building. The smaller buildings weren't locked, which surprised me. They were dormitories, and conveniently, they all had plas panels above each door.  They gave his drones a view of the interior of each room without having to enter them.  So much for privacy.

Only half of the rooms were occupied, a total of a dozen people, all of them asleep.  Some of the other rooms showed signs of occupation, with rumpled bedding and discarded clothing, but they contained no personal effects.  Where had the people who slept there gone?  And more importantly, were they likely to come back and cause a problem for us?

Strike withdrew his drones from the accommodation blocks and sent them outside to scan the land around the complex, to see if he could get any clues to where those people had gone.  There was no sign of them immediately around.

He sent the drones north, skirting the base of the mountains.  And there, in a deep gully, he found bodies.  Six humans were sprawled there.  "I don't think they've been there long," he said.  They all wore lightweight camouflage clothing, and had been carrying packs.  That explained the lack of personal effects in the rooms.

"They're in the sub-arctic and inadequately dressed," Bahar said.  "Is that what killed them?"

Strike zoomed the drones' cameras in on the still bodies.  "There are burn marks on their necks and heads.  They've been shot," he said.

"Were they trying to escape?"

"Stupid way to run if they were. They should've gone south."

"Then the rangers would've noticed them. They were probably trying to escape them too," Howin said.

"Anyway, think we found the missin' people," Rance replied. "Let's get back to the mission."

"Which just got a little easier," Strike said. "Because now we know the missing personnel aren't going to come rushing in to see their buddies. Let's go check out the big buildings."

He got his intel drones into the biggest building. He sent one of the repair drones in with them, and got it to melt the lock off the door of the big room inside. The bot pulled the door open, and the small drones followed it in.

"Medical stores," Strike said as the repair drone wrestled open a locker door. "More supplies."

"Yes, but what's in that inner room?" Bahar asked.

"Let's go see." There was another keylock, and Strike got the repair drone to deal with that too.

When he sent the drones inside I saw it was a medical suite, with six stations. At least this time there weren't any cubs on the platforms.

"Okay, so what're they doing there?" Howin asked. "Any evidence of behaviour modules?"

"Good question. Let's look." Strike sent the maintenance

drone to check the storage bays on the long wall of the room. Most held ordinary surgical supplies, but a small one had a new keylock on it.

"We'll just get into this one," he said. "Find out why they closed it off."

The lock flashed lights and beeped alarms. "Enough of that," Strike said, and wrenched it apart with the repair drone. The boxes inside the locker were stamped with a familiar logo.

"Programme supplies," Bahar said. So she'd recognized the logo too. Her scent had turned angry.

"Which means?" Howin asked.

Strike got the drone to undo a box and take out one of the shrink-wrapped modules inside. "It means that these are behaviour modules, and this is another offshoot of the Programme."

"What about cubs?" I asked. "Are there any here?"

Strike sent the drones to search the rest of the facility, but to my great relief, he could find no trace of any cubs.

"Does that mean these people just got here, or they killed every cub they took?" Rance asked. He smelled of anger.

"I don't know. There's nothing more to discover here," Strike said. He sounded subdued. If he was human I'd say he was depressed. "Let's go look outside. I've notified Kamaria Security about this installation. They're sending a team over in the morning."

He took his drones outside the complex, then locked the exterior doors of the accommodation blocks, and scrambled their keypads. "That should keep them inside until Security can round them up," he said. "Let's go hunt in the mountains."

He sent his drones at low altitude close to the mountain wall, to look into the mass of fissures and gullies there. He found nothing new on their flight north, and turned them south. 10.6 minutes' flight south of the complex they showed up something pale in a deep gully. "Going in closer," he said.

"Bones," Bahar said as the drones hovered over the pit. "Lots of bones."

"Small bones," I replied.

"Recording the site for evidence now," Strike said as he moved the drones in close to examine the bones from every angle. "Getting the maintenance drone to pick some up for analysis."

The heavier drone moved in and delicately picked up six bones, clasping them in its manipulators.

"And… coming inboard now," Strike said, and brought them into the shuttle. "I'll put these into an evidence box. I'm moving you south now. There's a cave you can spend the rest of the night in."

He sent a map to the shuttle's wallscreen. I didn't think

anywhere would be big enough to hide the vehicle, but I was wrong.  When we arrived I realised the rock opening was huge. Strike used the thrusters in delicate bursts to turn the shuttle around and ease it under the overhang of the cave while he sent his drones in to survey it.  Bahar peered out of the viewport and said, "It's more like a cathedral than a cave."  I had no idea what one of those was.

"Not quite," Strike replied.  "You're not completely hidden from the outside, but I can put the stealthing on if we need it."

I felt the jolt as the shuttle touched down.  There was no evidence of humans or their gear here.  I was surprised at that. The space was huge, and would make a good hideout.

"What are those black things?" I asked.  The drones zoomed in on the creatures, which were hanging upside-down by their feet from the cave roof.  What a weird way to rest.  Why didn't all the blood rush to their heads and make them feel dizzy?

"They're bats," Bahar replied.  "They could be harmless fruit-eaters, or they could be vampires."

"What are vampires?" I asked.

She told me about the creatures in human stories.  Humans really are weird, inventing that kind of stuff.  But she said vampire bats were real, and we needed to stay aboard the shuttle to stay safe from their bloodsucking.

I had no intention of going outside anyway.  I was tired and hungry, and really needed to sleep.

When I woke Strike had some bad news for us. "I've analysed one of the bones we picked up. I extracted its DNA and compared it with Snap's stored genome. It comes from a lion. I did an estimate of the number of skeletons in that pit." His voice went quiet. "They've killed over forty of them."

"Bastards!" Howin snarled. Her anger-scent spiked, making me sneeze.

"The other piece of news is better. Planetary Security have gone in and arrested everyone at that facility. They're now in cells on Itamarr. A Judiciary team is on its way here to take charge of them. I've filed full reports. That should get the facility shut down."

"So are we done here?" Howin asked.

"We are. Now it's time to find out what Rhian's up to."

And hope that she's not connected to that project, I thought.

# CHAPTER SIXTEEN

WE SLEPT UNTIL NOON local time, waking to a bright day. As we ate Strike updated us on things here. "Judiciary have been and gone," he said, "they've taken all the project people off-planet. They say to face trial. Let's hope they're genuine. I think they are, because they sent in the forensics bots to sweep that facility. The bots only left there half an hour ago."

"That's good," Bahar said. She took another bite of her trail bar. "So what's next?"

"What's next is talking to Rhian."

My head came up and I asked, "Where is she?"

"She's working on the grassland south of Valin Ranger Station. She's using a cave in the mountains down there there as her base."

"What else?" Bahar asked. "You're not telling us everything."

"Snap won't like this."

"Tell me," I demanded.

"She's tranking cubs and crating them up, then taking them back to those caves."

"Then what're we waiting for?" Howin demanded. "Let's get over there and ask her what the hell she's doing."

"We're going," Strike said, and woke up the shuttle's systems. He eased it slowly out from the overhang into a dull grey day. As we flew south rain began to fall. He switched on the stealthing as we flew over Valin Ranger Station, and I wondered what else he knew that he wasn't telling us.

The day dried up as we approached the location of Rhian's cave, and the clouds parted. Strike landed us behind the meagre cover of a rock projection close to the mountains. "Alert," he said. "A shuttle's just dropping into atmosphere. It belongs to a small cruiser called the *Questa's Gold*." I didn't bother asking how he knew that. He'd obviously hacked their coms. "Shuttle's armed."

"Who do you think they are?" Bahar asked.

"Most likely they're linked to the Programme," Rance snarled.

"I don't know." Bahar wasn't convinced. "They usually use Collective vehicles. This is civilians. It might be something different."

"Like a local gang boss muscling in?" Howin asked.

"It has to be a possibility," Strike replied. "I think we need to find Rhian before they do."

Strike lifted the shuttle and took it close to Rhian's cave base. He sent out the drones, then restored the shuttle's stealthing. There was a narrow ribbon of trees running south from this cave, along the base of the mountains.  At least there was some cover here.  That could be good or bad, of course.

Strike split his intel drones up and sent one group into the trees.  The rest he set to search the grassland.  The ones in the trees showed no signs of people having been there.  He sent the drones on the grassland up high, to get a longer-range view.

They brought us images of a skimmer and a cluster of figures in the middle distance.  He moved the drones closer, and I saw there were crates around the figures.  Oh, yeah.  We really needed to know what these people were doing.

One figure was readying dart guns.  Strike moved the drone in close, and I recognized the face.  "That's Rhian," I said.

Nearby was a cluster of spiny scrub, the only cover and shade for a long distance.  "Can you see what's in that scrub?" Bahar asked.  Her scent had turned anxious.

I had a good idea what would be there, and my guess was confirmed in 2.1 minutes.  A lion cub's head popped up above the grasses.  "There are cubs there," I said.

"Where are the pride adults?"

"Off hunting," I replied.  Some of Strike's drones had seen them running after a long-horned grazer, intent on bringing it down.  "They're a half-hour run from here."

Rhian finished her dart loading and approached the thicket. Three small heads revealed themselves, and the cubs began hissing at her. She tranked them with three swift shots, and as soon as they were asleep she went in to get them.

She lifted them up gently, cradling each sleeping cub in her arms, and laying it carefully into a crate, straightening out its neck and legs so that it slept in a good position.

"She cares," Howin said. "This isn't a vicious raid."

"Agreed. But she's still snatching cubs," Strike said. "We do need to find out why."

Rhian's team finished their work and carried the crates carefully into the skimmer. "Now we see if she really is using that cave as her base," Strike said.

He tracked the skimmer with his drones, and yeah, it was going to those caves. As it got close he said, "Alert. The shuttle that just dropped into atmosphere is coming over this continent now."

It came in over the eastern coast of Toral island, straight across the grassland towards the mountains. It was flying low, and going slow by the time it reached the place where Rhian had tranked the cubs.

"Think they're looking for traces of people," Howin said.

"Yeah. Agreed. Was just gonna say that," Rance replied. "And the first place they're gonna go look is that nice big cave system. We need to be prepared for a fight here."

The troops got into their armour. That was a tricky operation in the cramped confines of the shuttle, but Strike didn't want anyone going outside. The shuttle's stealthing was on, and he didn't want to turn it off and risk us becoming visible to the newcomers – at least, not until he chose to show our strength.

He sent his drones into the cave Rhian's team were using. They had a couple of crates of medical supplies there, and in a smaller cave beyond the squeeze of a wall they had sleeping rolls. To my intense relief, I saw no medical facility. But that just added to the question of what Rhian was doing with the cubs.

If she'd wanted just to do health checks on them she could've done them on the sleeping cubs out on the grassland. No, there was more to this, I was sure.

The troops had managed to get themselves armoured-up, and by that time the incoming shuttle was nearly on us. It was definitely civilian, and had a large and ugly logo of a melting gold shape painted on it. The name *Questa's Gold* was badly written in unevenly-sized ornate letters beneath the weird logo.

"Amateurs," Strike scoffed. "Is that supposed to be a gold bullion bar?"

I had no idea what one of those was. I knew humans coveted gold. I've never been able to work out why. They can't eat it, and it was only of value when exchanged for something else. There was so much about humans that I just didn't get.

"Snap, you get your armour unfolded," Strike said.

Oh, right. He planned to send me out there too, did he? I triggered the seal-up, and as I lifted each foot to let it fold around my paws I thought back to that mine on Reeva. The last time I'd gone in to rescue someone I'd come up against a Predatorbot. I'd witnessed its handler end its life by triggering its kill switch. I really, really, hoped I wouldn't come up against one of my own kind this time.

I thought about the pit of bones Strike's drones had discovered in the mountains here. No, these people probably didn't have Predatorbots. Because they'd killed all the cubs they'd been working on. Assuming that the people on the *Questa's Gold* were connected with that operation. We were about to find out.

My anger surged, and I snarled. It's a good thing my armour's coms were off. An angry Predatorbot was not what the team needed right now.

"That shuttle's landing right outside Rhian's cave," Strike announced. "People are getting out. Six of them, and I think they're armed. Out you go, people."

Strike opened the airlock door, and I let the troops exit first. Howin and Rance led a dozen of them out. The last of the newcomers had just disappeared into the overhang of the caves, and the troops ran to catch them up. Strike sent his drones back into the cave as I galloped along behind the troops.

"Be careful," Bahar said over our team feed. She was fretting back on the shuttle. Strike had prepped the med bay there. That was adding to her anxiety. Strike was anticipating casualties. Nobody answered her. We were all focused on getting into the cave.

The feed from Strike's drones showed me Rhian and her team were taking the crates with the cubs in them out of their skimmer. As she unloaded the last one, the first hostile entered the cave.

"Oh. Definitely armed," Strike said as he swung a rifle towards her.

"Hand those over!" he roared.

"Who the fuck are you?" That was one of the men on her team. He'd produced a pistol from his pocket and pointed it at the hostile.

"He's wearing only light armour," Strike said in our feed. "Need to get a move on, team."

Howin and Rance disappeared into the cave. I followed them in. Strike's drones recorded the troopers taking down the hostiles with one well-placed shot to each back. All except the mouthy one, who ran for the cover of a large stalagmite.

Howin swore as he started firing towards Rhian's team. They had their heads down and were running full-pelt for the cover of the skimmer.  My heartbeat thundered as I watched the hostile target Rhian.

"Not gonna let you get away, yer bitch!" he yelled.  "Yer ruined everythin'.  I could'a been rich."

"Bastard's got himself into cover," Howin said.  "Going in now."

I hissed as she ran in front of the stalagmite.  Things happened fast then.  The hostile saw her coming and fired off another shot towards Rhian.  My heart was thundering.  I couldn't stop him.  I couldn't do anything to keep her safe…

Howin took down the thug.  As he dropped she called, "Rhian?  You okay?"

"No," a feint voice called from the other side of the skimmer.

Strike sent his drones round there.  "Trouble," he said.  Rhian had fallen onto her front, and blood was running down her back, a frightening amount of it.

"Emergency medipack, now!" Howin ordered.  Running feet sounded, going away from us.  "Anyone else hurt?"

Nobody was.  They all stood there, numb with shock, looking down at Rhian leaking blood.

The troops returned with the medipack and Howin and Rance got Rhian into it.  Its systems powered up as the lid closed over her, and Howin checked the readouts.  "Bad, but still alive.  She has a chance," she said.  "Let's move.  We need to get her into the shuttle's cryopod." *Coming aboard now, Strike,* she said over our feed.

*Acknowledged,* Bahar said as Rance and the troops eased the medipack around the side of the skimmer. As they took off with it back to our shuttle Howin straightened up and addressed the rest of Rhian's people.

"You her team?" she asked.

"Yeah, we are." The woman's voice was soft and shaky.

"Take those cubs to Valin Ranger Station. You know where that is?"

"Yes, but they don't know we're doing this," one of the men said.

Stupid humans. This wasn't the time to worry about that. "They will know about it by the time you get there," Howin said. That sounded like a threat. It was, in a way. "Get the cubs out of here, tell the rangers what happened. Those thugs came from a shuttle, and somebody's going to come looking for them before long. You don't wanna be here then. Go!"

Her barked command cut through their shock and paralysis and they scrambled to get aboard the skimmer. Howin took cover behind a stalagmite while it took off. As it disappeared out of the cave she said, "Time for us to go too."

I felt wobbly as I ran behind the troops back to our shuttle. How did stupid humans ever think that fully-emotional

Predatorbots would make the perfect fighting force?  They didn't think, that was the problem.

As I galloped along behind the troops my fear was out in full force.  Rhian looked bad.  She'd lost a lot of blood.  What if she didn't survive?

# CHAPTER SEVENTEEN

I WAS LAST TO GET aboard the shuttle, and as soon as I was in the airlock Strike closed the outer door behind me and lifted it off. We went up fast, and I had to struggle with the sloping deck while I got through the inner door and into the passenger compartment.

The troops had retracted their helmets and were strapped into their seats. All except Howin, who was standing over the cryopod. She was bracing herself with both hands against the wall, fighting the near-vertical ascent. Her attention was on the cryopod's readouts.

I could have accessed those readouts direct with my processors, but I was afraid to. What if they told me Rhian was dying? I remembered Strike calling me The Cowardly Lion. I was definitely that again right now.

Howin stirred, and turned away from the cryopod. "She's under," she said as she flopped into her seat. "That's all we can do for her right now."

That didn't mean she'd survive. It meant Howin didn't know if she would.

I retracted my armour's helmet and settled down on the deck as Strike's voice came through the nodes. "New trouble," he said. "The *Questa's Gold* is coming my way. I'm going to have to move. Sorry. It means you're going to take longer to reach me."

"We can't afford any delays," I snarled.

"Rhian's in suspension. She'll be fine until we wake her up. A little extra time getting to me isn't going to make any difference. Staying out of the way of that ship definitely will."

Strike's tone was sharp, and it punched through my building panic. He was right. We did need to stay out of the way of that trouble. For Rhian's sake.

"Come to the control room, Snap," he said. "I could use your extra pair of eyes."

"On my way," I said.

There wasn't much room to turn around in the shuttle's passenger cabin. The damned thing had been designed for two-legs humans, not big, four-legged lions. I stood on someone's foot as I turned around, but they didn't complain. Howin gave my rump a pat as I eased into the doorway.

The control room was just as cramped, even though Strike had taken out one of the seats in there to give me space. I settled down on the floor as Strike put the nav plot up onto the screen. *Thunderstrike* was ahead of us. He'd have to do another orbit to intercept and pick us up. Which was all very well, but the display showed that the *Questor's Gold* was gaining on us.

"You're stealthed," Strike said. "It shouldn't be able to see you."

"But the ship's armed," I replied.

"Yes." Strike's voice was quiet.

We both knew what that meant. The newcomer might not be able to see us, but the stealthing didn't repel missiles. You needed shields for that, and they would flare on impact and give our position away.

Strike had come to the same conclusion. "You're going to do an atmosphere-skip," he said over the com. "Get strapped in, Howin."

Oh, right. This was going to get rough. I lay down on the deck, putting as much of my body in contact with it as I could.

Then we were diving into the boundary between space and the planet's atmosphere. You had to get the angle just right for an atmosphere-skip, and hope that nothing was coming up to meet you on the other side of the planet. It was a fast way to close the distance between us and *Thunderstrike*, but not without risk.

This planet only had one spaceport, which was behind us. Hopefully that meant nothing would be coming up into orbit where we emerged.

The deck dropped out beneath me, then 6.5 seconds later it rose again, slamming hard into my body. I was glad I still had my armour extended. We continued diving and rising for 4.6 minutes, and despite my armour my body was feeling bruised from the violent motion. The hull thrummed around me, and one particularly vicious skip sent a series of deep thuds along the port side of it, moving from bow to stern.

"How much longer?" I asked.

We did have a military-grade shuttle, and in theory its hull was built to withstand this kind of treatment, but it still made me nervous.

I knew Strike would be worried about it too, but he'd never let me see that. But when this was over there'd be a request for me to go and smell the soundness of the shuttle's hull before we took it out again.

"Coming out now," he announced over the com. The noise around me abruptly died. The nav display re-calibrated, and I saw *Thunderstrike's* icon not far from our position. "Damn! *Questor's Gold* is moving up on me. Damned ship has too much power to be genuinely civilian."

That… wasn't reassuring. "Can we get aboard in time?" I asked.

"Just." The shuttle's engines went to full power. No, Strike was red-lining them. Or knowing Strike, even more than red-lining them. I hoped the shuttle would hold together long enough for us to reach him.

"This is getting monotonous," Bahar said.

She was referring to what happened to us when we left Reeva on our last rescue mission. Our shuttle was attacked that time before we could reach the safety of *Thunderstrike*.

"Not going to do that this time," Strike said.

*Thunderstrike's* hull came up in front of us. It was all sweeping curves, with huge wings with guns on them fixed to his port and starboard sides. Warmth coursed through my body at the sight of it. This was safety. This was home. If I could only get aboard in time.

A red light flicked up on the console in front of me. The drives were overheating.

"Only a few more seconds," Strike said as the vehicle bay airlock loomed large ahead of us. The outer doors slid open and Strike cut the shuttle's drives. The red warning light went out as the engines stopped. Strike engaged the thrusters and put the shuttle down onto its pad, playing them to settle it perfectly into its spot as if nothing was wrong. My irritation rose again. We had a badly wounded woman here. We couldn't afford this fancywork.

Relax, Snap, I told myself. Rhian is in cryo. She isn't deteriorating. She's alive.

"Get your armour sealed up," Strike said over the shuttle's com. "I want to keep this bay in vacuum until I've checked that engine over."

That made sense. I triggered the seal-up of my helmet, then got myself out of the control room. By the time I got down to the bay the troops had all disembarked. Howin was at their head, guiding Rhian's cryosled into the inner airlock.

It took a frustratingly long time for us to clear that airlock. Strike had to pressurize it again before letting us through into the ship. My gaze kept going to the cryosled's display, but I didn't want to read that data.

I let the troops go up in the lift first, taking Rhian to the med centre. As it came down again and opened its doors for me Strike said, "Get a move on, Snap. I want to lock this down."

Oh, right. He'd keep the vehicle bay in vacuum until his bots had checked the shuttle over, but doing that put unusual stresses on the rest of his hull. He wanted to put the deck seals down on the lift shaft. Which he couldn't do until I got above them.

I stepped into the car and the doors closed behind me. Before I could turn around the car was in motion. It let me out on Deck Two, and I retracted my helmet. *Lift seals in place*, Strike said in my feed.

There was a long-running debate among humans about whether machine intelligences were capable of love. That was just humans refusing to acknowledge what they'd created. They were good at that. Of course machine intelligences felt love.

Needing to keep the people they loved safe was one of the ways they showed it.  That was behind Strike's need to put the deck seals down now.  We were perfectly safe, and he knew it, but he still felt the need to do that.

*Rhian's in the med unit*, he said over our private feed line. *Should know how bad... Oh, the* Questa's Gold *has just found me.*

Over the ship's com he said, "Alert.  Microjumping now."

We disappeared from the real, and reappeared a few minutes later.  "Firing," Strike announced.  The thrum of the hull told me he'd fired his port wing guns.  Another series of thuds 10.6 seconds later was the starboard wing guns firing.

"Jumping."  Strike's voice was sharp.

I braced my body against the hallway wall as reality disappeared, then reappeared.  4.6 seconds later the wing guns fired again.

"Oh, now we're trying missiles, are we?"  Strike's voice was calm.  "Countermeasures launched.  You're going to have to get something newer than that, buddy."  He sounded almost amused at the attack.  "And... missiles exploded.  Moving in."

He jumped again, and again the wing guns fired, both sets together this time.  "Got it," he said.  "Weapons systems disabled.  They might have some damage to their drives too."

I expected him to go in for the kill, but instead he said, "We're done here. We're leaving." There was a savage tone to his voice. Strike frightened me at moments like this. He was leaving that disabled ship to fail. Which meant a slow death for its crew. This was how Strike showed his anger.

*Why did you do that?* I asked over our private feed line as we ran for the jump point.

*I stripped the ship's logs when it first appeared. They're raiders. They specialise in the capture and sale of rare wild animals. I've just checked the Starnavy's files on the ship's crew. Arrest warrants have been issued for six of them on seven different stations, relating to habitat destruction on ten planets.*

*Oh,* I said. Strike had done that for me. It was his own kind of rough justice. It made me feel uncomfortable. *You shouldn't have...*

*It's done now.* His tone told me he wasn't prepared to debate the matter. *Now let me concentrate if you want Rhian to live.*

That was emotional blackmail, and it told me he was upset. I dropped the subject. Strike could perfectly well have argued with me while he controlled the med suite to treat Rhian, but there was no point in getting into a fight with him about it.

"How is she?" I finally found the courage to ask.

"She's lost a lot of blood, and has damage to her liver, but she'll live. I'll make sure of that," he said.

# CHAPTER EIGHTEEN

DESPITE STRIKE'S FIERCE DECLARATION, I was still worried about Rhian. I knew that losing a lot of blood was never good for any organic being.

I went to *Thunderstrike's* control room, and Strike let me in. Bahar was in the captain's seat. "It's good to see you all got back safely," she said.

"Yeah, but Rhian got hurt. We didn't do it properly," I replied.

"Sometimes you just can't make things go like you want them to."

"I'm scared," I admitted. "What if she dies?"

Bahar slid out of her seat and came to kneel down in front of me. She put her arms around my neck and pressed her smooth cheek to my furred one. "It'll be fine, Snap," she said softly.

"If her sisters are in this much danger, how much more danger is Nyla in? Does she know it? What if these attacks on the sisters are being done by someone in the Collective? Maybe they're not isolated attacks. Maybe they're part of one big plan, and they…"

Bahar squeezed my neck. "Breathe, Snap," she said. "Deep breath." I complied. "Good. Now another." I felt calmer after a couple of minutes. "That's better." She released me and stood up.  "You were panicking.  Panic never helps anything."

"True, but Snap's made a good point, though," Strike said quietly.  "I hadn't considered that someone in the Collective might be co-ordinating attacks on the sisters."

"Why should you?"  Bahar dropped into her seat.  "They've never had anything to do with the Programme."  She sounded calm, but she smelled worried.

"The Programme's just got a new Head.  Maybe he's driving the search," Strike said.

"That would be a nasty, vindictive thing to do," Bahar replied.

"It fits with the Programme's objectives, then," I said.

That shut them up.  The silence lasted for 1.7 minutes.  Strike broke it.  "I hate to admit it, but Snap could be right.  And if the Programme is actually hunting the sisters then we need to figure out their strategy, and step up our search for them."

Bahar threw her hands in the air.  "We're clutching at straws.  We've got lucky so far.  What if the other sisters aren't so easy to track down?"

"I need to use more resources to look for them, but that means telling more people in the Unit about our plans.  So far, I've kept to a small core of contacts I know I can trust.  Going wider carries more risk.  Remember Chan?"

"How could we ever forget her?" Bahar replied.

Chan had been the machine intelligence of the Collective

frigate *Firechan*. She'd turned traitor to the Unit a while back. She'd helped to launch a code attack on Strike which had nearly deleted him. Strike had become a lot more wary about trusting our contacts since then.

But we couldn't operate without that intelligence network. He was going to have to trust someone.

"Anyway, our first step is to get to Xalvador Station and get Rhian healed by the medics there," Strike said.

Bahar and I exchanged a look. We were both thinking it depended on Rhian surviving that long, but neither of us was willing to voice the thought.

"And I know you're too scared to ask, but she'll survive," Strike said. "I've synthesized blood for her. It won't do the job as well as her real stuff, but I don't have the tech to bulk her own blood up. The stuff I've put into her will keep her functioning okay for a short while. And at least it won't leak out again now I've sealed up the holes.

"The liver regen I can do, and it's under way. There's nothing more I can do to help her now, which is why we're running for jump as fast as we can."

Oh, right. While I'd been panicking about Rhian Strike had been quietly getting on with his job. That was the way machine intelligences showed their love for people too.

"Sorry," I muttered.

Bahar looked down and stroked my neck. "For what? For feeling fear and concern? Never apologize for that, Snap." She paused for a moment. "Sometimes, I think you're more human than I am."

While Strike made his way out to the jump point most of the troops got into cryo suspension. Strike thought that we could meet trouble on Xalvador if the *Questor's Gold* had buddies there who knew what we'd done to the ship. So he kept Howin, Rance, and five of the troops awake.

The others got into their cryopods just before Strike took us into jump. As soon as we were through Bahar did her usual trip to the cryobay to inspect their pods.

Strike had got to the stage where he didn't even comment on her obsession now. I wasn't sure whether it still upset him though. He'd just stopped talking about it. I was sure I'd find out how he felt sometime.

We downjumped at Xalvador Station into a chaotic situation of traffic warnings and a very busy-looking nav plot. "Has something happened here?" Bahar asked.

"Getting updates now," Strike said. He changed course. "Yes, it has. There's been an attack on station. Nobody's claimed responsibility for it. It was a ship hit-and-run, and the ship was stealthed."

This wasn't a good situation for us. We needed to get Rhian into the medical facilities here swiftly. And we needed those medical facilities to be safe.

"What if it's our raider friends?" I asked. "You did say the *Questor's Gold* was upgraded. Maybe their friends have done the same with their ships."

"It's a possibility," Strike conceded. "We won't know until Security have done their analysis.

"Getting Security briefing now. They're unsure who's responsible for the attack. All the suspect ships jumped out and they don't anticipate any further trouble. Three sections of Level Three are in vacuum, and locked down. Fortunately, there's no loss of life. Just a dozen minor injuries. But that's the reason for the traffic chaos. Everything's being diverted away from those sections."

"Another delay," I said. "We really didn't need this."

I began to worry about Rhian again. Strike had said the artificial blood he'd given her would be fine for 'a short while'. How long was 'a short while'? Would we get Rhian into station's medical facilities in time?

# CHAPTER NINETEEN

STRIKE REQUESTED PRIORITY DOCKING at Xalvador Station, and got it. But it meant he had to weave his way through six different incoming lanes of ships to reach his assigned dock.

He was on high alert as he began his complicated journey into station. We were changing course every few minutes, descending and rising out of the way of slower-moving craft. As we made one tricky course change he opened a private feed line to me.

*Be ready to come into my architecture, Snap,* he said.

*Why?*

*I think Traffic Control's coms are compromised. I fear an attack.*

That… wasn't good. The last code attack Strike had suffered nearly succeeded, and I'd nearly lost my best friend in all the universe. And Strike couldn't cut off contact with Traffic Control. He needed that constant data to get through these ships safely, and…

*You're panicking, Snap. Stop it. It doesn't help.*

Then I felt something try to contact me. *My processors are recording an attempted contact,* I said. *Oh, they're searching for my behaviour module.*

*Run your disguise code.* Strike's voice was sharp.

*Yes, of course. Running it now.* I set the code Strike had written for me in motion. He'd created that code when he removed my behaviour module. If anyone knew I was a Predatorbot and tried to contact me, it would return reports of a damaged and uncontactable module. Strike thought we should keep secret the fact that he'd removed it.

The contact with me stopped, and I said, *They've gone away.*

*They'll assault me directly now.*

Was that fear I heard in my friend's voice? Yes, it was. Strike could be killed, just like us organic beings. And he feared death, just like the rest of us.

*Check my coms and auxiliary memory storage*, he said.

I slipped into his architecture through the pathway he opened for me. This was different from when we shared good experiences together. I had no sense of his shipbody and of the forces of the universe on it this time.

I had tightly-focused access to his coms and auxiliary memory storage only. The block to the rest of his systems registered in my mind as a solid wall. It told me he was worried about me being a danger too.

His auxiliary memories rarely got used. Strike had had them installed to future-proof his shipbody, in case getting tech and supplies from the Collective got difficult in future.

I checked the memory contents.  The files were what I expected, run codes for filing and retrieving stored data.  Strike had written some detect code for me, which I sent off to search for hidden code bundles.

My search of his auxiliary memories turned up no malware or faults.  *I can't find any hostile code*, I reported.

*Good.  Stay in there.  We're burning into dock.*

I kept a watch on the coms system as he changed course again.  That was the weak point.  He was right, he couldn't shut down the Traffic Control datalines.  To my intense relief, I saw nothing hostile coming through.

12.4 minutes later Strike said, *We're at the dock.  You can come out now.*

I withdrew my awareness from his architecture and lay down on the deck.  6 seconds later I was asleep.


I woke to Bahar slapping my cheek.  It stung, and I snarled at her.  She left me alone, and slipped back into her seat.

I lifted my head.  "What did I miss?" I asked.

"Not much," Strike replied.  His voice was soft and warm.

"Are you all right, Snap?"  Bahar's voice was anxious, like her smell.

"Just exhausted."

"You're staying here while we get Rhian ashore.  You're in no fit state to prowl station's hallways," Strike said.

"And whose fault is that?"

"Yeah, okay.  But I needed you there.  Thanks, Snap."

"What are you two talking about?"  Bahar sounded exasperated.  She usually reserved that tone for when we were fighting about something.

"I needed Snap's help to ensure no hostile code got into my systems," Strike said.  His firm tone implied 'I am not going to discuss this issue'.

"Oh," Bahar said, and wisely dropped the subject.  "So who is going ashore with Rhian?"

"Howin, Rance, and our five awake troops.  And no, I don't think that's overkill."

"So I'm staying here?" Bahar asked.

"Yes.  Rai's putting drones up over our troops.  She'll give me access.  Go to the rec area and get yourself some coffee.  I'll stream the drone images on the wallscreen there.  You'll be able to see what's happening."

That was Strike's way of saying, 'Don't hassle me, but I know why you're fretting.'

Bahar followed his suggestion, and I struggled to my feet. I felt weak, and dragged my paws as I followed her out of the control room.  Walking along the hallway woke me up.  It stretched my spine, and the movement sharpened up my sluggish mind.

The drone images were on the wallscreen by the time we reached the rec area.  Howin appeared outside *Thunderstrike*, tugging on the cryosled's tether to get it to follow her down the ship's ramp.  Rance and the troops followed her.  Strike opened the berth lockout gate for them, and they stepped onto a busy dock.

The troops closed in around the cryosled, and Howin set a punishing pace along the dock towards the lift lobby.  I always found it surprising how she cleared people around her out her way without actually bumping into them.

She was tall and broad, and was wearing armour, but so were many of the other people on this military dock.  Somehow, Howin had a presence which screamed 'don't mess with me'.  The subtext was 'get out of my way', and people usually did.

She carved her usual swift path through the swirling chaos on the dock, and the troops reached the lift lobby in record time.  A car was being held for them there by Rai, its display panel reading 'Medical Priority'.  As Howin approached with the cryosled the car doors opened.

She guided the 'sled into the car and the troops followed, accompanied by Rai's drones.  Rance pushed out a chancer who tried to get into the car with them.

As the lift hummed into motion Howin asked, "Did he tag you

with anything?"

"Can't see that he did on the video," Strike replied.  "Rance, check your armour."

"Already doing it," he said.  "Not showing up any bugs."

The lift stopped and the doors opened.  The drones whisked out, going to check the hallway beyond the lift lobby.

"Alert," Strike said.  "Three armed men coming towards the lobby."

An image from the drones came up on the wallscreen.  Three men were stalking down the hall.  They were rough-looking, with weather-beaten skin and long, tangled black hair escaping from untidy braids.  They were dressed all in black, their pants and jackets fake leather; shiny, and too tight.

They wore leather holsters with pistols in them.  The weapons banged into their legs as they walked. One of the drones zoomed in on them.  "Oh, they're Yankling pistols," Strike said. "Ancient."

'Ancient' in Strike-speak meant the tech was more than five Standards old. "Rai's reported them to Security. They're on their way."

The men wore their jackets open, revealing black T-shirts beneath them.  "Anyone recognize that graphic?" Strike asked.

"Isn't that Outlier Action?" Bahar replied.

"Checking. You're right," Strike said.  "But I think these three are something else."

Howin did too.  She ordered the squad to surround the cryosled, and they strode forward out of the lobby.  The men in black increased their pace down the hallway.  "Something's not right here," Strike said.  "Howin, expect attack."

"We are," she replied.

The troops didn't have their helmets deployed, and that was a concern, but the quickest way to trigger a station alert was to go around in sealed-up armour.  You drew attention to yourself if you did that, and we were trying to do the opposite here.

As Howin guided the cryosled into the hallway the three men spread out across it, blocking the squad's progress.  This time, Howin's magical ability didn't clear them out of the way.  "Definitely something wrong there," Strike said.

"Out of the way!" Howin roared.  "Medical priority."

Slowly, the men moved over.  As Howin tugged the cryosled past them the lead man looked down, trying to see the face beneath the 'sled's lid.  Fortunately, it was completely frosted, and he could see nothing of Rhian's features.

"He's looking for someone," Strike said.  "I knew there was something wrong about them.  Rai's sent the video on to Security.  I'm sure they can haul 'em in for something.  My feeling is those T-shirts are disinformation.  Not a good choice here, though.  That organisation isn't popular on this station."

"Maybe it's the Collective trying to put the blame for this on that rebel group," I suggested.

"That's nasty," Bahar said.

"It's a regular way they work, though," Strike replied. His voice was laden with contempt.

If ever you wanted to know why Strike went rogue, why he created the Special Investigations Unit, here was your answer. He hated this kind of deception by the Collective.

Bahar called Strike a 'naïve idealist'. He believed in democracy. And he believed that the people who'd been elected to make life better for others ought to actually deliver on that promise. When they didn't, it angered him, and he worked against them.

New drone images came up on the wallscreen. "Rhian's reached medical admissions," Strike said. "Oh, that's Gitsuka. Good."

Gitsuka was one of our human Unit contacts on Xalvador, a medic on station here. Bahar had once joked that with the Unit's diverse range of skills they could set up in government themselves.

I've rarely heard Strike as angry as he was then. He'd told her that wasn't his purpose. His purpose was to see that honesty and decency ran the Collective. Strike's heart of gold had a hard edge sometimes.

On the video, we saw Rian's cryosled disappear into a triage room.

"So, she's reached Medical.  All we can do now is wait," Strike said.

# CHAPTER TWENTY

BAHAR AND I WENT to sleep while the medics worked on Rhian. I was exhausted after being in Strike's architecture, and from all the tension on-station. I slept for ten hours.

I woke, yawned, and said, "Feed me, Strike."

"Then go to the galley, messy cat," he said. There was no humour in his voice. He sounded tense.

I went to the galley, and he fed me a haunch of falacca meat. I'd expected him to update me on things while I ate, but he said nothing. I opened a private feed line to him and asked, *What's wrong?*

*They put Rhian into an intensive body-cleanse programme. Gitsuka said they had to get every bit of my artificial blood out of her."*

*It makes sense.*

*I did what I could!*

Oh, right. He was upset about this. *Yes, you did*, I replied. *They're not criticising you by doing that.*

*It feels like it.*

*Do they always do that when they're changing someone's blood?*

*I don't know.* He went quiet for 5.1 minutes. *Yes. Gitsuka says they do.*

*Then it's nothing to do with what you did at all.*

*Thanks, Snap.*

*You're welcome.*

Bahar appeared in the galley then, demanding to be fed a solid breakfast. "So what's next?" she asked when Strike had printed her meal.

"I'm not sure."

Bahar and I exchanged a look. Strike was never not sure about the next action. I hoped he wasn't having a crisis of confidence. I wasn't sure I could handle that.

"I need your input on this. I'm considering calling another Unit meeting. We can reach a lot of our Outlier contacts from here. If we think the sisters are out there somewhere, those contacts could help us to find them much quicker. But…"

"But you're afraid of running into another Chan," I said.

"Exactly."

"So how can we stop that?"

"I need to review each contact before I invite them. Check their recent history."

"That sounds like a lot of work," Bahar said.

"It is. It'll take me hours. But it's something to occupy my mind while they're working on Rhian."

Strike set his checks in motion right away. As well as reviewing local contacts' activities for the last five Standards, he also checked into their contact networks. He was doing this thoroughly, which told me how scared he still was about Chan's betrayal.

In the end he invited three hundred contacts to the meeting, half of them machine intelligences. The conference was scheduled for five hours' time. But before that, we needed to talk to Rhian.

Gitsuka said that medical wanted to release her, but she felt we should talk to Rhian first. She was confused, and didn't know what to do next. That wasn't surprising, given that she'd gone to sleep on a planet, and woken up on a station a long way away.

So Bahar and I agreed to go to meet with her in a room in the medical facility. The nervousness I'd felt when meeting Fia rose again now. And I didn't even talk to Fia, others handled that conversation. This time, I was going to meet her sister face-to-face. And if she knew that Nyla was dead...

Stop it, Snap. That isn't helping. You need to know the truth. Whatever it is.

We left *Thunderstrike* at mid-Second Shift. I was wearing my armour, but it was retracted. I'd changed the camouflage pattern again. This time it was displaying a design in shades of red. I'd copied the logo on it from a popular petbot manufacturer, and tweaked it to be similar but bogus.

Bahar looked tense as we came down *Thunderstrike's* ramp. She wore wine-red trousers and a matching tunic, both devoid of all decoration. She'd got wary of displaying her tribal finery since she'd been kidnapped. She smelled anxious.

Strike had arranged with Gitsuka to hold Rhian in the medical facility 'under observation' until we talked to her. They hadn't told her the details of what had happened to her on Kamaria, so it was up to us to do that.

Gitsuka had found us a secure room close to the medical unit. She said it was where station Security took suspects for interview once medical had patched them up. We got there safely, and Gitsuka met us in the admissions room and introduced us to Rhian. My heart was hammering as I followed Bahar into the secure room.

Rhian was older than Fia, and had more weather-beaten skin. Her white complexion had a dark tan. She had long copper hair, and was shorter than I'd thought. Drone images always distorted things like that.

"Hello," Bahar said as we walked into the room. "I'm Bahar, and this is Snap. We're from the Collective frigate *Thunderstrike*. We brought you here from Kamaria. I gather medical haven't told you the details of that?"

"They said you froze me down. The last thing I remember was

getting shot in that cave."

"You were in a bad way, so we brought you here to get expert medical help."

"Thank you.  I don't know what to do now."

"If it helps, the illegal project on Kamaria has been shut down," Bahar said.

"Thank the Universe!  They kept snatching cubs and they never came out of there again."  Her green eyes glinted with anger.  "I thought they were trying to set that damned Programme up there.  I was snatching the cubs away to safety to stop them."

My body sagged with relief.  I'd been 98% certain that was Rhian's motivation, but now I had it confirmed.

"They were trying to set the Programme up again," Bahar said. "We stopped that."

"Good.  What happened to the people on my team?" Rhian asked.

"They're still on Kamaria.  Collective Security moved in to arrest the bad guys.  Your team are rehabilitating the cubs they grabbed.  The Collective Assembly is pushing through protected reserve designations for two-thirds of the planet.

"That's brilliant news!  They don't need me back there, then. Which leaves me with the problem of what to do next.  And no money to get anywhere."

"We could help with that," Bahar said. "Do you know where your sisters are?"

Rhian shook her head and made an exasperated noise. "No. Me and my big mouth. When I learned about Nyla's involvement with the Programme I went ballistic. It triggered a massive argument between all us sisters. We haven't spoken since."

I felt a massive surge of disappointment at her words. I still didn't know if Nyla was alive.

Bahar exchanged a look with me, and I nodded. "What I tell you next has to remain confidential. Do you agree to that?"

Rhian looked startled. "Yes, of course. I always keep my word."

*Are we secure here?* I sent over my private feed line to Strike. *We are*, he confirmed.

"Nyla didn't know the full truth about the Predatorbot Programme until someone on the inside leaked the data on behaviour modules to her. I'm told she went ballistic then, and demanded their removal. She was told she was hired to be a researcher, and that she needed to just shut up. That's when she resigned from the Programme, and she later leaked the details."

"The Collective wouldn't like that," Rhian said. "Is she safe?"

"We don't know. Nobody knows where she is right now. She made herself scarce after outing the Programme. Wisely, I think.

We've tasked ourselves with finding all the Vatan sisters and making sure you're in places of safety. But right now, the only other one of you we know the location of is Fia. She's on Davion. A while back she was snatched by a bunch of raiders who grabbed several of the colonists. They wanted to make them into mining slaves. We got them out. Fia's just got back to Davion."

Strike had received that notification two days ago. He said he hadn't thought it would take her so long to get home. He'd fretted about it.

"Is she safe?"

"She is now. Davion is a wildworld, and it wants to stay that way. We used what we'd learned on Kamaria to push the Collective to designate reserves on Davion. The colony's leaders want to make their wealth from wildlife tourism.

"All of which is a long way of saying you'd have plenty of work if you wanted to join your sister on Davion. And our next mission takes us out that way, so we could take you there." Bahar laughed. "If you knew how often Starnavy frigates got used on civilian courier missions you'd rename us. Anyway, our next mission takes us past there, and we have approval to take you there – if that's what you want."

It was Strike's suggestion to talk about warships doing civilian runs. Sometimes we forgot we were supposed to look like part of the Starnavy.

Rhian sighed. "Yeah, I should do that. It's long past time I ate humble pie and made up with them. I did try to contact everyone a Standard after I blew up, but nobody responded. I thought they'd cut me off. It could get awkward on Davion if Fia doesn't want to talk to me." She shrugged, and smiled a twisted smile. "I'll just have to deal with that, won't I? Okay, I accept your offer of transport."

"Right. Good. We need to make some arrangements before we're ready to leave. We'd like you to stay in medical until I collect you. There are Outlier Action gangs roaming the hallways here. We don't want you getting caught up in that trouble."

"I don't want to get tangled up with them either. I've already had a couple of run-ins with those thugs. I'm happy to stay put until you come get me."

"Good." Bahar stood up. "We're going to a briefing now, but I expect we'll be able to move out before the end of the day."


Bahar and I left the medical unit then. There were Security teams patrolling the hallways as we walked to the lift lobby. A very large and very obviously armed Security operative was stationed in the lobby, a visible deterrent to trouble there.

Despite the heightened tension, we got back to *Thunderstrike* without any trouble.  Strike let us aboard, and we went to the rec area.

"So, it went well," he said as he produced coffee for Bahar.

She took the cup and slumped into a seat.  "Better than I expected.  The line about acting as civilian couriers worked well.  I'll remember that for future use."  She sipped her coffee.  "It's good that she wants to re-establish contact with her sisters, but it's frustrating that she doesn't know where they are."

"That would've been too easy," I replied.

# CHAPTER TWENTY ONE

THE UNIT MEETING STARTED a station hour later.  Strike put up the avatars of the attendees on the wallscreen in the rec area.  He'd expanded it to cover the whole of the biggest wall. Bahar clutched another cup of coffee, which she was working her way steadily through.  I sat down beside her, trying not to feel nervous.

Strike was moderating this meeting.  "Welcome to the Unit briefing," he said.  "I've been concerned by recent reports of unrest in the Outliers, and I'd like your assessment of the situation.

"I and my crew have recently had some run-ins with thugs from Outlier Action.  They seem to be getting stronger, and that's a particular concern.  With that in mind, let's start with a report from Teiga Station.  What's the situation around there, Ruusu?"

"It's getting tense," Ruusu said.  She was a black-skinned human woman with a worried expression.  "We've had several Outlier Action rallies on Naretha, some of them turning violent." Naretha was a planet near Teiga Station, an outlier of the Outliers.

"What's driving things there?" Strike asked.

"Outlier Action are actively recruiting.  I suspect they think their main chance to break away from the Central Worlds is approaching, with the upcoming Presidential election. But there are many colonists who don't want to be separated from the Collective. There's a fair bit of opposition to them, and Collective Security has now prioritied shutting down their rallies."

"That's going to lead to serious conflict at some stage," Strike said. "Has anyone else noticed the growth of Outlier Action?"

The picture our contacts built up was worrying. In system after system Outlier Action were present. They'd started out in the Zurrial Triangle, and were steadily working their way Centralwards. They were keeping off the Central Spine route up to now, though.

*We need to decide what to do here*, Strike said over the feed to Bahar and me as the last report came in. *Outlier Action are becoming a serious threat. I think we need to redefine the Unit's purpose.*

*What've you got in mind?* Bahar asked.

*Let's discuss it with them*, Strike said. He returned to the meeting feed and said, "I'm concerned that Outlier Action might be a serious danger to the Collective. I formed the Unit to be a check on the Collective's excesses, but at least the people setting the Collective's policy directions are elected by everyone."

That 'everyone' included sapient machine intelligences.

Strike had been forbidden by the Starnavy from actively campaigning for sapient machine intelligence voting rights, but he'd been influential in several unseen ways in helping to get that vote passed.

Sapient machine intelligences had had the right to elect Assembly members and vote for the President for over twenty Standards now. And they had local voting rights on the station or planet where they were installed.

At first there'd been a lot of human opposition to giving them that right. The usual scaremongering of 'machine intelligences will take over' got ramped up into a serious fear campaign. The stupid humans didn't realise that sapient machine intelligences had had the capability to control everything for thirty Standards before the vote was passed. They'd had a long time to make humans into their slaves if they'd wanted to. It hadn't happened.

Humans never did understand that sapient machine intelligences needed positive relationships to survive. They'd never been natural killers, thanks in large part to the ethics and morals databases which every one of them received before wake-up. But also because most machine intelligences simply liked most humans.

The Collective was a democracy, however creaky its systems were. Outlier Action was a collection of thugs and chancers, and we really didn't want them grabbing power.

"I'm proposing, in view of what we've heard here today, that we widen the Unit's remit," Strike said. "I would also like us to work to ensure that Outlier Action doesn't grab power where their people aren't legitimately elected.

"I recognize that you are only a small part of the Unit, and I will be sending out communications to every contact later today, asking for their views. But as a start, I would like to take a vote from you people. Do you agree to that widening of the Unit's remit?"

The vote went Strike's way. Only three 'no's' came in, and Strike dealt with those by asking the contacts to remain in the Unit and only work on issues covered by its original remit. They agreed.

I found all this legal stuff tedious, but Strike said this was the basis of democracy. If the Unit was dedicated to supporting democracy then it ought to be democratic itself.

"Well, our suspicions have been confirmed," Strike said when the meeting ended. "Outlier Action is growing fast. I'm not sure whether we should take Rhian to Davion now."

"We've promised," Bahar replied. "And what about Fia? If she's in danger there then we need to intervene."

"Yes, you're right. Go get Rhian. I'll be happier when she's on board."

Howin and Rance had gone back into coldsleep as soon as we docked, so Strike arranged for one of our human Unit contacts in Xalvador Station Security to escort Bahar and me to the medical centre and back to Strike.

The hallways were quiet on our way to the medical unit, and the journey was uneventful. When we arrived there Rhian was ready to go, clutching a pack someone had given her with a few changes of clothes.

We got back to *Thunderstrike* without any problems too, and Bahar settled Rhian into a room in Strike's crew quarters.

I went to the control room while Bahar fussed over her. "Okay," Strike said as I walked in. "Let's get under way before something new erupts."


We didn't have a priority line out to the jump point this time, and it took us three shipboard days to reach it. As we lined up for jump Strike received a Starnavy update. There was trouble in the Johar Cluster. The message was a muster order to go there.

We really didn't want to get diverted there, so Strike sent out a garbled 'message not received' reply, and deleted the data from his files. Then he went into jump before anyone could send him the orders again.

The jump to Ataret Station was long, and I fretted about what we'd find when we reached Davion.  Was Fia safe down there?

I was in my usual space in the control room as Strike approached downjump.  Bahar sat beside me in the Captain's seat.  She seemed tense, and she smelled anxious.

Strike had suggested that Bahar wore her uniform, in case we were contacted.  She rarely did, but now she had put on her most worn field uniform.  It was always a shock to see her with Captain's stars on her shoulders.

I didn't know much about her Starnavy history before she'd joined Strike's crew.  She'd never talked about her past.  Anyone who tried to get her to talk about it got brushed off with 'That's the past.  Let's focus on what we need to do now.'

"Downjump in three… two… one…"  Strike did that smug thing of cutting off his com at the last microsecond again.

Then we were through into normal space, and immediately proximity alarms blared.

"Trouble," Strike said.  "Shields going up now."

# CHAPTER TWENTY TWO

"GETTING A SITREP," STRIKE said. "We've got Outlier Action trouble. They're trying to make a hostile boarding of Ataret Station. I've been ordered into a squadron to defend it."

"I guess we can't refuse that," Bahar said.

"No, we can't."

"So where are we going?"

"To this location." Strike flashed up a position marker on the nav plot. "Which means a tricky bit of manoeuvring in."

I could almost detect excitement in Strike's voice. He loved the challenge of difficult manoeuvres. What he didn't like was the idea of killing people at the end of them. Bahar said that centuries ago he would have been labelled a conscientious objector. She said that many humans had been executed for that stance.

So Strike needed to keep his objections to killing secret. There was always a risk that he'd be uninstalled if he defied the Starnavy. Yes, people were still getting killed for their objection to killing.

"Jumping now," Strike warned.

Reality smeared, then came back again. Bahar gasped when we emerged. We were close in to station.

"This is our assigned position," Strike said. His tone was defensive.

"They just didn't expect you to jump in here," I replied.

"Station's under attack. We can't waste time. Weapons hot."

"Will you two stop it," Bahar said. "This is no time for bickering."

"Snap, keep your attention on this cluster of ships." Strike flashed them green on the nav display. "Nobody's sure who they are."

"No beacons?" I asked.

"You got it. Request to turn them on's been made. It's been ignored."

That likely meant raiders. I settled in to watch that section of the display. Strike said my attention to detail was better than Bahar's. She tended to lose focus after a few minutes. I could keep my attention locked on the plots for hours. Strike was monitoring them, but at times like this he always wanted me to act as his backup.

He thought my ability to keep focused came from the lion's hunting skills. After all, lions would never eat if they couldn't patiently watch their prey.

"That group of ships is definitely incoming," I said. "Four of them."

"Yeah. I just got detailed to go meet 'em," Strike said.

"Moving out now."

He took us in a long curving arc below the station and up on the other side. There were fewer ships here, and I wondered if that was part of the attackers' battle plan. Maybe they were trying to keep everybody engaged between station and the jump point, leaving this area free for their reinforcements to come in. Nice try, but it wasn't going to work.

"*Starspear* and *Firefury* are coming to join us," Strike said. "We have orders to turn those incoming ships away from station. They're still refusing to switch on their beacons and answer hails. Now tagged as hostiles."

"Weird that they haven't announced themselves," Bahar said. "If they're Outlier Action you'd expect them to be blabbing."

"There's a different feel to this," Strike said. "More professional."

That… wasn't reassuring.

Strike waited until his wingships arrived. He was quiet for a while, and I realised the ships were talking. I always found that frustrating. Although I was part machine intelligence I couldn't follow a pure machine intelligence conversation. They were just too fast for me.

"Okay," Strike said. "Got some intel on those ships. They are Outlier Action. They came in from Warrun. They were trying to attack that station too, but were driven off. With any luck, that means their ships'll have some weaknesses from their previous engagement. Oh, we're getting a broadcast now."

"This is Commander Diamond, Outlier Action Strike Force Ten. Stand down station's defences and prepare to be boarded."

"Negative, hostile force." That was a machine intelligence's voice, calm and firm. "We will defend against hostile action."

"And… station's guns going live now. Adding those no-go zones to my tactical map," Strike said.

That would make combat messy. Sometimes I wondered how he kept track of all the variables.

"Hostile One approaching. Moving to intercept," he reported.

I watched the plot as he moved, expecting the whole cluster of hostile ships to go to weapons hot and attack together. Instead, one ship came on ahead alone.

"I'm guessing that's our so-called Commander Diamond," Strike said. "A martyr in the making."

I've never understood why people got themselves killed for a cause. It seemed like a stupid waste of your life to me. You couldn't change things if you were dead.

"Starnavy ship, stand down." The man's voice had a little less bravado to it this time.

"This is the Collective frigate *Thunderstrike*. Be advised that we are ordered to defend Station. Those orders authorise the destruction of your ship if necessary.  Back off.  Traffic Control have sent you a line out," Strike replied.

"We have no intention of leaving," he growled.

"Incoming," Strike reported as warning lights came up on the console.  "He's launched Clusterfire missiles.  More old tech.  Countermeasures away."

Strike blew the missiles up close to the raider.  "Hopefully the blast and debris will do him some damage.  Jumping," he said.

He came out of the microjump behind the raider, and I heard his big fin guns fire.  The raider's engines exploded.  "Jumping," Strike said again.

When he came out of the jump the raider was a burning hulk.  "What happened?" Bahar asked.

"Friendly fire.  His buddies shot at me.  Except I wasn't there."  Strike's voice had a flat tone to it.  Another machine intelligence had been killed, and he hated that.

I had to admit Strike's tactics were clever.  Strike really didn't want to kill, and this way he'd got the rebels to do the killing instead.  But now those buddies were coming for us.

It was three ships on three ships, and as the hostiles spread out Strike and his two wingships settled into one-on-one dogfights.  Well, as much as leaping about in space could be described as a dogfight.

The ship Strike engaged had a competent crew, and to judge from some of their moves their crew or machine intelligence had seen Starnavy service.  Strike took several hits to his shields. They briefly died under a barrage of energy fire, knocking out one set of thrusters.  That was inconvenient, but not life-threatening.

"Annoying," Strike said as the shields came up again and he jumped away from the raider.

He came out behind it and fired immediately.  Something blew up amidships.  "That's the weapons control module gone," he said.  "They can't shoot at us now."

The local Commander's voice came over the com.  "Stand down attack.  We're taking this bunch in for interrogation."

"Acknowledged," Strike said.

"We're receiving docking instructions," he told us.  "Let's get into station before something else erupts."

# CHAPTER TWENTY THREE

"RECEIVING LINE IN NOW," Strike said.  "Fortunately, we're on the right side of station.  Which is useful, seeing as I have two dead sets of portside thrusters."

"You'll need to get those repaired," Bahar said.

"Already arranged.  Fortunately, we have Unit contacts in the Starnavy shipyard here.  They've scheduled our repairs.  I don't expect anyone will object, given we've just saved the station."

Bahar laughed.  "*Thunderstrike* saves the day.  Again."

"Well, I did."  Strike sounded huffy.

Bahar pointedly didn't reply to that.

"Okay, so I did have help," Strike admitted after 2.6 minutes.

Bahar laughed.  "*Thunderstrike* the humble!  I never thought I'd see the day."

"And you tell me off for bickering," I said.

Bahar looked surprised at my comment, then she nodded. "Okay, maybe that was mean.  Sorry, Strike."

"On our way in to dock," Strike said.  I noticed he hadn't accepted Bahar's apology.  He didn't chatter like he usually did on the way in, and I began to get worried about him.  I secured a private feed line and said, *What's wrong, Strike?*

*Nothing.  I'm just concentrating.*

*A massively smart machine intelligence like you doesn't need to concentrate to do a simple docking.*

My mixture of flattery and mockery got through to him, and he laughed. *Bahar dismissed my actions out there*, he said.

*No, she didn't. She admires what you did. She didn't say it very well.*

*It doesn't seem like that.*

*You know humans. Half the time I can't work out what they mean. They have to make things so complicated.*

Strike laughed again. *That is so true.*

Over the com he said, "We're on final approach to dock. We've been ordered to a briefing on-station about the attack. Or at least, Bahar has. I think she'll have to go alone to this one. Let's hope it doesn't result in us getting orders we've no intention of following."

A local hour later we docked at the shipyard. I stayed in Strike's control room. Bahar put on a better uniform, and went on-station to the Starnavy briefing. Strike would have a line into the meeting. He'd show me what went on there.

He fed me before it started, then I joined Rhian in the rec area to watch the briefing. Strike said they wouldn't discuss anything classified, so it was okay for a civilian to listen in. I'm sure the Starnavy Commanders would disagree with that, but I didn't bother to argue. Strike had made up his mind, and that was that.

The wallscreen lit with a view of a huge lecture theatre. It was only a third full of bodies, but the wallscreen behind the stage displayed 98 avatars.

A tall black-skinned woman with her hair braided and pinned tight to her head strode to the podium.

"That's General Nenge," Strike said. "So, we have high-level involvement here." Was that a tinge of worry I heard in his voice? I think it was. Why was this action worthy of her attention? We were about to find out.

The briefing was tedious. Rhian wandered off to grab coffee several times during it. But at the end of the session we'd learned that Outlier Action were growing into a big and organized group, and that they were getting stronger.

No surprises there, then. To our intense relief, *Thunderstrike* was ordered to stay here and to run patrols around the local system. By sheer good fortune, the three ships also assigned to that duty were also members of the Unit. That would make things easier.

Strike had told us that the vote on extending the Unit's brief to deal with Outlier Action had gone overwhelmingly his way. Nobody wanted unelected tin-pot dictators, as Bahar called them, taking power. Strike had chided her for using what he said was an ancient colonialist expression, but he'd agreed with her anyway.

The thing we hadn't expected was the broadcast from the Collective President that came at the end of the briefing. It was rare that President Jorrak did an all-Starnavy address. Maybe he was tending to his image. It was too late for that. He was already disliked by a large part of the Collective's population. When he came up for re-election he'd have a real fight on his hands.

The camera showed him in an office somewhere on a Central world. Strike said that he worked out of several spaces, and kept moving between them in irregular patterns. That had cut the assassination attempts down massively.

The plas windows behind him were darkened, giving only the faintest view through to tall buildings beyond. It could've been an office in any city of any Central world. Which, I guessed, was the idea; so hostiles couldn't fix his location.

The President stood in front of the windows. He was white-skinned and tall, in his sixties. His black hair was styled in waves, and reached to his shoulders. He wore a bright blue silk suit. Bahar called him vain, and said she was sure he dyed his hair.

"I wanted to address our loyal Starnavy troops today because you 'deserve to know what you're fighting for," he said.

"We're not fighting for anything. Yet," Strike said. "I don't like the sound of this."

"We are facing the biggest threat to our democracy, to governance of the people by the people, that the Collective has seen in its long history," he said. "That threat comes from an organisation named Outlier Action. Their sworn purpose is to 'free the Outliers from the Collective's control and neglect' as they term it."

"I will admit that there are many challenges to governing such a vast and far-flung collective of worlds like ours, but I assure you that we have never neglected the Outliers.

"The Assembly has authorised the use of whatever force is required to deal with the threat of this organisation. For many of you, that will result in redeployment to more far-flung systems. I am sure you agree with me that, while democracy has its flaws and challenges, the right to choose one's ruler is preferable to being governed by someone with no legal authority. If Outlier Action were to succeed in wresting power from your duly-elected representatives, then all of you would be affected by that move.

"You will all be receiving new orders in the next few days. I look to the Starnavy, Landforce, Air Defence, and the Seanavy to keep us all safe in these challenging times."

*Creep*, Bahar sent over our feed line as the screen blanked. *What prompted that?*

I suspect we're about to find out, Strike replied.  Get back to me fast.

# CHAPTER TWENTY FOUR

IT TOOK BAHAR A station hour to get back to *Thunderstrike's* berth in the shipyard. She arrived half an hour before the techs assigned to repair Strike's damage.

As Bahar settled into the Captain's seat Strike said, "Fia contacted Rhian an hour ago. They want to re-establish contact. Fia's invited Rhian down to stay with her. She's one of your kind, Bahar." Strike meant that Fia was aromantic asexual. "I suspect Fia will be glad to have the company of her sister – at least, for a while."

"That's all very well," Bahar said. "But we're not going anywhere until your repairs are done."


Strike needed two sets of repairs. There were his portside thrusters to replace on his shipbody, and the Xenophon shuttle needed its slagged drive fixing.

One group of techs went to the bow portside hold, to deal with all the connections to the thrusters. A second bunch went to the big vehicle bay to start work on the Xenophon.

None of these people were part of the Unit, and I could sense that Strike felt uneasy about having them aboard. He wanted me to stay in the control room. He said he didn't want anyone knowing there was a Predatorbot aboard.

That was unnecessary fussing. He'd locked off his lifts, and those people couldn't get to his upper decks anyway, but I did what he wanted. Strike put feeds from the two bays, and an exterior view of his thruster area, onto the wallscreen for us.

The thrusters were being worked on by repair bots. I could sense Strike's nervousness as he watched them approach his hull. Had he always seen everything as a potential threat? No, I don't think so. Trust for strangers died in Strike after Chan's attack on him.

That should've made him into the perfect paranoid warship. Instead, it had made him into an anxious person who found it hard to function without reassurance at times.

I watched the repair bots uncouple the big thruster assemblies. They worked slowly, and their grapple arms looked too delicate for that work.

"First set's free," Strike said as the bots eased the large chunk of metal carefully away from his hull. The feed from inside the hold showed the techs accessing the diagnostics panel on his hull wall. The hard connections for the power and data feeds to the thrusters were made in between the inner and outer hull layers, so the only eyes-on view anyone had of the coupling-up process was via the cameras installed in that space.

I hadn't understood why Strike needed all those hull layers

when I first came aboard. It was only after he'd given me his 'Dangers of Space' presentation that I'd understood. I'm a lion. Lions don't have to worry about running out of air anywhere they live.

I guess that means I live an unnatural life, locked up inside Strike's hull, but let's face it, I've never had anything that could be described as a natural life for a lion. I was grown in an artificial womb, bioengineered to speak and not to reproduce, implanted with memories and processors which make me half machine intelligence. No, I've never been a natural creature.

The bots got the second set of thrusters safely uncoupled, so I switched my attention for a moment to the techs in the vehicle bay. They wore EVA suits. They'd come in from the external airlock, and the bay was in vacuum. It didn't seem to bother them working in suits, and all the heavy work was being done by the repair bots anyway.

After a short inspection, the verdict was that the Xenophon's engines were slagged beyond repair. One of the antigrav units had been hit too, so that would also need replacing.

They got to work installing the new units straight away, taking the opportunity to upgrade the shuttle's engines. But that meant Strike would have to install new software to run them. I saw a lot of Strike anxiety happening in my immediate future.

5.4 hours later all the work had been done.  As the techs left Strike said, "I need to do full system checks now.  And…"

"And you want me in your architecture, checking for hostile code," I replied.

He was quiet for a second, then said, "Well, I do."

"Then let's get on with it.  Where do you want me to look?"

He sent me a listing of possible locations where hostile code could lodge.  It wasn't restricted to the propulsion systems.  He wanted me to check all his shipbody.  Strike really was bothered about these changes.

He opened a pathway for me and I slipped into his architecture.  This time I was into his whole shipbody again.  It felt different from how it was in the deep black.  The port side of his hull registered the cold of space.  The starboard side, locked onto station, was warmer.

Stop sightseeing, Snap.  You have a job to do.

I worked my way down Strike's list of locations, sending the seeker code he'd written for me in to check for anything hostile lurking there.  I didn't find anything.  Strike didn't find anything either on his parallel checks.

I withdrew from his architecture, and by the time I returned my attention to the control room Strike was checking his thrusters out with the techs.

The Xenophon's engines took a lot more checking, and by the

time their installation was done I was thoroughly bored – and hungry again.

Strike wanted me to go into the Xenophon's architecture and check for hostile code there too. He fretted that they might've hidden trackers in the new engines. So I went into the shuttle's architecture and checked out his propulsion suite. Strike had already done it, this was just him wanting reassurance. He hadn't found anything wrong, and I didn't either.

"No trackers that I can find," I said.

"I think we're okay," Strike replied. "But the real test will be when I do the shakedown. That'll be tomorrow morning. Station can't clear enough space for us until then."

While I ate in the galley, Bahar escorted the techs off Strike's shipbody, then came up to the control room. When I'd finished eating I joined her there.

"Well, that's done," she said. "We're all fixed and ready to go into danger again."

"Not funny, Bahar," I said.

"No, I suppose it wasn't." She sighed. "But it might be true with these Outlier people about. What's next on our agenda?"

"I need to take the Xenophon out on its test flight before I trust people to it," Strike said.

"That makes sense," Bahar replied. "Which means we're

kicking our heels around here for a good few hours yet."

"Then you can do something useful with your time and go meet our local contacts," Strike replied.


Bahar and I went on station in the early evening. Bahar had chosen to wear a blue tunic with tribal decoration embroidered onto its front and sleeves. I was pleased by the move. It meant she was getting over her kidnapping.

We were going to a café half-way round station's ring from Strike's berth, so I'd opted to wear my armour. I'd set it to display the same pattern as Bahar's tunic. She laughed when she saw it. "The perfect petbot. Come on, Snap," she said. "Let's get out there."

We emerged onto a quiet dock, and the lift system was quiet too. But when we reached Menagerie, all that changed.

The café was noisy and busy. Menagerie was a place which welcomed all types of avatar. Which was good, because both our contacts were machine intelligences. Tyger's avatar was a tiger with an iridescent coat of blue and silver stripes. Raptans's avatar was a silver eagle.

Bahar ordered dinner, and after it had arrived Tyger said, "We've been monitoring activity from Outlier Action recently. They're becoming more than a civilian protest unit."

"How so?" Bahar asked.

"They've acquired some ex-Starnavy senior officers in their command structure recently," Raptan said.

"We think their hunting strategy is to recruit as many ex-Starnavy people as possible.  We've flagged them as trouble."

# CHAPTER TWENTY FIVE

"HUNTING STRATEGY?" BAHAR ASKED sharply.

"Sorry.  Investigations Unit slang.  Didn't mean they were killing people, but targeting people with useful skills and experience."

Bahar's scent shifted to worried.  I was a little too.  That could make Outlier Action a serious threat in future.  I wondered if it was part of Jorrak's plans to hang onto power if he lost the upcoming Presidential election.

Our contacts said the station felt tense.  Bahar decided she didn't want to get caught up in something here, so as soon as she'd finished her meal we made our way back to *Thunderstrike*.  Her anxious smell was becoming stronger.

When we arrived at the dock where Strike was berthed it was busy with techs scurrying about in groups.  They had an air of urgency to them.  Bahar increased her pace, striding along the dock fast, forcing me to trot to keep up with her.

We reached Strike's berth without challenge, and Strike let us aboard.  "Glad you're back," he said as we stepped into the lift.  "Come up to the control room.  I've learned something important."  He sounded serious, and that always worried me.

The lift let us out on Deck Two, and Strike opened the door of the control room for us. "So what have you learned?" Bahar asked as she plopped into the captain's seat.

"A Regulus Lines ship got blown up at Zirali Station half a Standard ago. They think by Outlier Action. The report's only just got here."

Bahar's scent spiked to fear, and I had to sniff to stop a sneeze. "Why did it take half a Standard for the report to get this far?" she asked. "Are the ansibles down somewhere?"

"No. Somebody didn't pass the report on."

"So why is this bothering you?" I asked.

"Because one of our contacts told me he'd met Zana Vatan a couple of Standards ago. At that time, she was working as an officer on a Regulus Lines freighter. He didn't know if she still worked for them, though. But if she does, it's likely that she's in the Outliers somewhere."

"On an unarmed ship, with Outlier Action throwing their weight around. That's not good," Bahar said. Neither of us voiced the thought we both had. Had Zana been on the ship which was destroyed? Now my scent was as anxious as hers.

"I've tried to follow up the report, but I'm getting nowhere," Strike said. "And we can't go anywhere right now anyway. The best thing you humans can do is go sleep."

Bahar and I followed Strike's suggestion. He said Rhian had

already gone to her cabin. I went to my quarters and tried to settle to sleep, but it came hard. My rest was fretful, and I woke up several times, my blankets in a tangle, thinking about Zana. Strike played white noise in my cabin to soothe me, and eventually I sank into a deep sleep.

When I woke Strike fed me, and I gobbled up the sweet meat swiftly. I was very hungry, and couldn't stop myself drooling over it. When I'd finished he said, "Go keep Bahar company, messy cat, while I clean up here." He was scolding me again, and that was a good sign.

"The Xenophon launch is in an hour," he said as I padded down the hallway. "We're undocking from station now."

When I walked into the control room Bahar was already in her seat. This morning she wore camouflage field clothes.

"We already have our cargo for the Xenophon," Strike told us. "As soon as we've done the test we can load it up. I'm going to have to do an official test, so you'll have to stay out of my architecture this time, Snap. And… we're reaching our assigned test area now. Going inertial. Initialising Xenophon systems. Wish us luck, people."


The test went perfectly, and no faults showed up. I hadn't expected any, but to judge from the relief in Strike's voice when he said, "All clear," he obviously had.

He brought the Xenophon back into the vehicle bay, then he had the task of loading the cargo he'd stored there. He lowered the blast wall which divided up the bay and his bots got to work loading up.

That took a couple of hours, and while it was going on Strike continued his journey to the jump point. I thought he seemed tense, but we met no problems on the way out.

The jump was short, and we came out five shipboard days later. We were all relieved to see that Davion wasn't under attack.

"Looks quiet here," Strike said as he eased into orbit. "Shouldn't have any problems today."

"Famous last words," Bahar replied.

She'd had to explain that one to me. Why do humans twist up their language so much? It was hard enough for me to learn it without that cleverness.

It was night on Fia's hemisphere when we came into orbit. We debated whether to wait until dawn to contact Fia, or send her a message now.

Bahar argued for a message. She said it would give Fia some advance notice, as she put it. Humans make communicating so complicated sometimes.

So Rhian recorded a message, and Strike sent it down with his com codes. "Now all we can do is wait," he said. "Most likely she won't reply before morning."

Strike arranged for us to land at the regional shuttleport close to the villa complex where Fia lived.  There was a Unit machine intelligence in Traffic Control on Davion, and she'd see that the Xenophon was safe while it was on the ground.

Rhian fidgeted all the way down.  She was used to shuttle drops, so it had to be the prospect of meeting her sister again which was making her nervous.

We came in over the nightside of the planet.  As soon as we crossed the terminator into daylight Strike said, "That's Vermidion Ridge.  Fia's villa is the big white one on the edge of the cluster.  And we're setting down at the shuttleport you can just see in the distance.  You'll have to take the skimmer to her house.  Final approach now."

The shuttleport was smallish, but as well as a dozen hardcrete landing pads it also had a runway.  They got old-fashioned landers here too.

Strike took us down on the antigrav units, lowering the shuttle neatly onto its assigned pad.  "A perfect flight," he said.  "No problems at all."

"That's good to know," Bahar replied.

"I've told Fia you've arrived.  She's expecting you all."

Strike powered-down the shuttle, and Bahar led us into the big storage bay.  We got into one of the smaller skimmers.  It didn't look so obviously armed and threatening.

"Off you go," Strike said as Bahar started it up.  He opened the big airlock door onto a bright morning.  "They're pathetically excited to get the medical stuff I've brought.  They want to unload my holds right away."

"If you were in pain and you needed drugs to stop that pain you'd be pathetically grateful too," Bahar said as she steered the skimmer out of the bay.

"Oops!  Done it again, haven't I?  I just don't get this pain thing," Strike said.

Bahar steered the skimmer along the shuttleport's exit road. "Think of it as a malfunctioning circuit.  It interferes with your smooth operation, so you can't ignore it.  It's a malfunction that's always there, messing things up."

"That wouldn't be good," Strike conceded.  His voice, coming from the skimmer's dash, was quiet.

"No, it isn't.  So you get those supplies unloaded a.s.a.p. Right?"

"Yes, Captain."  I couldn't decide from Strike's crisp response whether he was mocking her or not.

The settlement of Vermidion Ridge was nestled close to the range of low hills on the horizon.  Strike said it was a half-hour drive away.  The road there was long, straight, and boring.  But the scenery around the road was pretty.

We were driving through a vast area of grasses and wildflowers. Dots of red, blue, purple, gold, and white rose out of a sea of tall, frothy green. The wind blew through the grasses, bending them in one direction and then another, sending huge waves rippling over their surface. It was hypnotic, and I had to drag my gaze away from it.

Fortunately, Bahar was keeping her attention on the road. Not that the drive was challenging. Only two battered groundcars passed us on the journey.

Vermidion Ridge was bigger than I'd expected. A cluster of thirty houses, set in their own substantial plots of land, made up the settlement.

"They're smallholders," Bahar said. "Grow-your-own-food types. Well, we're here," she announced as she lowered the skimmer into a parking space beside Fia's battered groundcar. Both hers and Rhian's scents had turned anxious. I had stopped fretting about how this meeting would go. I could do nothing to influence the outcome.

Bahar unlocked the skimmer's doors. "You go ahead, Rhian. We'll go catch some air out here."

"Thanks," Rhian said, and strode off towards the steps leading up to the veranda which wrapped around the building.

Bahar got out of the skimmer and looked around. I joined her, taking in the scents, and the touch of this different wind on my face.  It was good to get the scent of human out of my nose.  "They call this prairie," she said.  "It's totally natural."

"It's beautiful," I replied.

She looked down and ran her fingertips along my neck.  I sensed she was surprised by my comment.  "Do you wish you lived somewhere like this?" she asked.

"No.  I wouldn't know how to survive here."

"Yeah. I guess we messed you up royally," she said quietly.

"You made me into something new," I said as she climbed the steps up to the veranda.

I suppose I should be angry about that, but I wasn't.  I had a good life with Bahar and Strike.

Bahar settled onto a weather-beaten bench with a soft sigh and looked out over the landscape.  "Now we wait," she said, and her anxious scent increased.


Fia came to get us a short while later.  She was dressed in battered and faded field clothes, and her hair had grown long since I'd first seen her in that mine.

"Welcome to Vermidion Ridge, Bahar, Snap," she said. "Come inside, and we'll catch up."  She smelled calm, and that was a good sign.

The interior of the house was covered in what looked like bits of tree. I'd never seen anything like it before. Polished wooden floors were strewn with rugs woven in bright colours. Couches covered in other bright fabrics were arranged around a low table made from what looked like a huge section of tree. I found it curious that humans used bits of dead plants to decorate their homes.

Fia bustled off, returning with a tray containing three glasses. "This is local Ridge brandy," she said. "Made by my neighbour. I thought we should celebrate us getting together again, Rhian."


Bahar and I returned to the shuttle at midnight. Fia had offered us places to stay for the night, but Bahar was anxious about the increasing tension in local space, and didn't want to risk getting cut off from *Thunderstrike*, so we decided to go back straight away.

Rhian had already settled in at Fia's house, and the sisters were busily recalling past memories while we walked out of the door. The reintroduction had worked just fine.

The drive across the prairie was like being in space. There was no light there at all. The only lights we could see came from the regional shuttleport we were travelling towards. Bahar's anxious scent increased as we made our way through the darkness.

We came onto the shuttleport's approach road, and she asked Strike, "Are you unloaded?"

"Unloaded, and distributed. We're ready to leave," Strike said.

"Good," Bahar replied as she steered the skimmer into the shuttle's airlock.

Strike closed it behind us, and we went through to the control room. As soon as we settled there he launched.

Our journey back to *Thunderstrike* was swift, and we encountered no other shuttle traffic. It was nice to get back to the ship without being attacked for once. "Bringing you aboard now," Strike said, and opened the vehicle bay airlock. He landed the Xenophon as neatly as always, and repressurised the bay. As soon as we had air we went up in the lift to the control room.

Bahar plopped into her seat and said, "That's the reunion done. It went well. The sisters are getting on fine. What's next for us?"

"Back to Ataret Station," Strike said. "We need to check out the situation there before we plan our next move."

# CHAPTER TWENTY SIX

ATARET STATION WAS QUIET when we downjumped there, and Strike got into dock swiftly.

He contacted Nuru, a human Unit member on station.

"Things are calm here now," she said, "so why don't you and Snap come ashore, Bahar?  We can take you to a swanky new eatery.  It's called Startail's Revenge."

"Sounds dangerous," Bahar said.

"It's good.  The revenge part is about a celebrated chef opening his restaurant here instead of in the Central Worlds.  They gave him bad reviews there.  Gangster bad vibes, we've since learned."

"Definitely sounds dangerous."

"Not at all.  And the food's divine."

Bahar laughed.  "Okay, you've sold me.  When and where should we meet you?"

"18.00 on Level Two, Section D-200.  We'll meet you in the lobby."

"Done.  See you later."


Bahar and I went on-station 3.6 hours before our dinner date. Bahar tried to look relaxed as she strode along the hallways, but there was a scent of anxiety to her. I followed her around the curve of the ring to a series of shops where she bought clothes, jewellery, and food, instructing the delivery bots to take her purchases to *Thunderstrike*.

While she did her shopping I sat outside, trying to keep still, like a good petbot. The keeping still was a real challenge for a predator, but if I followed everything that moved around me somebody would soon realise that wasn't normal petbot behaviour.

By the time Bahar had finished her shopping I was thoroughly bored. "Come on, Snap," she said. "We've time to get you fed before my dinner date. Maya's arranged for you to eat in her office." Maya worked in Logistics at Ataret Station, and she was part of the Unit.

"That's good. I'm hungry," I said.

Bahar trailed her fingers along my neck. "I thought you might be. Come on." Now her scent was calm. I think this is what humans call retail therapy.

We went to a logistics complex a little further around the curve. Maya met us there. She was a tall woman with skin as black as space, and a broad smile. She took us into her office and said, "Strike told me you like marissa meat, so I printed you that." She smelled of uncertainty, and maybe a little of fear.

"Thank you," I replied. "That's perfect."

She took Bahar through to the next door office, and let me eat in peace. The slab Maya had printed for me was pure meat, not an authentic haunch like Strike always gave me. I ate every bit of it.

She reappeared as I finished the last piece. "Good, you're done," she said. "Getting you to Startail's Revenge now."

The walk wasn't far, and as we entered the lobby of the restaurant there was no missing Tyger's iridescent-striped avatar pacing around there. Nuru was with him. She had light brown skin and short curly black hair. The concierge didn't seem happy about Bahar bringing her petbot into the restaurant, but eventually led us to our table.

We had a booth by the outer station wall, and a view of space through a small viewport. I sat down beside Bahar, and the humans ordered their meals. They smelled calm, for once.

I was full, and a little sleepy, so most of their conversation passed me by. I focused on them again when I heard the words Regulus Lines.

"We put out a lot of feelers," Helia said. "It's more difficult to get information when we can't make a direct request for it, as in this case. But in the end we got one lead.

"Our sources say Zana Vatan is still with Regulus Lines. She's the First Officer of the *Dreaming Galaxy's Light*," Nuru said.

"Do you know where the ship is now?" Bahar's eagerness showed in her voice. Her smell mixed hope and fear in a strong swirl of scent.

"Sorry, no. That sighting was when the ship was docked at Ralziel Station. It's over a Standard ago. But we do know the ship is working the Zurrial Triangle. Regulus concentrates its business in the Outliers."

"That's useful. Thanks, Nuru. Any lead's better than none."

We returned to *Thunderstrike* at midnight, station time. Fourth Shift had already started, and the dockside was quiet. Today Bahar had put on a tunic and trousers with modest tribal decoration, but she'd left her gold-decorated clothes and fancy jewellery behind.

Her body was tense as we walked to Strike's berth, and she smelled anxious, but nobody bothered us. We reached the lockout gate, and Strike opened it for us. As we trudged up the ramp and into the airlock, I thought Bahar looked as tired as I felt.

We stepped into the lift, and Strike said, "I know it's getting late for you two, but can we talk before you go to sleep?"

"Of course," Bahar said. "We'll come to the control room."

Strike took us up to Deck Two. The minty tang of his atmosphere sharpened-up my senses. Strike let us into the control room and Bahar plopped into her seat. I lay down on the deck beside her. It had been a long day, and my head felt heavy. I rested it on my front legs, and hoped that Strike's discussion wouldn't last long.

"So we know where Zana was a year ago," he said.

"I'm guessing from that you don't know where the *Dreaming Galaxy's Light* is now?" Bahar asked.

"Not yet. Regulus might be a civilian shipline, but their data encryption is top-notch."

"Which means it's taking you longer to crack it."

"True. But we have to start our search somewhere, so we'll start at Ralziel Station." Ralziel was part of the Zurrial Triangle, and a long way from our current location.

"Okay, that makes sense. Agreed," Bahar said. "Anything else you need us for right now?"

"Nothing important."

I yawned, and Strike said, "Go get some rest, sleepy cat."

"You wanted to talk," I reminded him.

Bahar stood up. "Hey, it's too late for fighting. Go and sleep, Snap."

"Out you go, sleepy cat," Strike said, and opened the control room door for us.

We stepped into the hallway and Bahar said, "Sweet dreams, Snap." She ran her fingers down my neck in a gentle caress, then turned towards her own quarters.

Strike let me into mine.  His bots had straightened-out my blankets.  That was Strike showing he cared again.  If Starnavy Commanders realised that their sapient warships cared more about their crews getting a good night's sleep than they did about killing, they'd have a meltdown.

I settled into my bed and yawned again.  I was tired, and full, and now I knew where we were going next.  "We're still only half-way through this quest," I said.

"Quest?"  Strike seemed startled by the word.

"Well, it is.  We're travelling vast distances to rescue women in danger."

"Don't let Bahar hear you describe it like that.  You'll get a long lecture on patriarchal rewriting of women's history.  Which totally happened, but it's far too late to tell you about that now."

I turned over onto my side and curled my legs up.  "Do you think we'll find Zana at Ralziel?"

"Who knows?  Tomorrow is another day, and we'll fret about it then.  Go to sleep."

I let my body relax.  We could find Zana.  We'd already found two of her sisters.  But  where was Nyla?  We still didn't know.

Strike was right.  Tomorrow was the day for fretting about all that.  Now I needed to sleep, surrounded by the people who loved me, the people I loved most in all the Universe.

"Goodnight, Strike," I said, and closed my eyes.

# COMING SOON

## OUTLIER ACTION

### Book 3 of the Thunderstrike Diaries

Strike, the sapient machine intelligence of *Thunderstrike*, has learned that Zana Vatan is the First Officer of the Regulus Lines' freighter the *Dreaming Galaxy's Light*.

He is reassured that at least one Vatan sister is safe. Then Regulus gets a new CEO in suspicious circumstances, and concerns for the shipline's safety grow.

Regulus Lines ships start disappearing, and Strike suspects their captains have joined Outlier Action. That group believes President Jorrak has abandoned the Outlier colonies to their fate. They have started attacking ships and stations, to acquire essential supplies.

Then ugly rumours of Regulus's new CEO sexually assaulting female crew members surface.

Zana is now threatened by attack from both Outlier Action and her own shipline's boss. Strike must find her fast.

# FALSE MANIFESTO

## Book 4 of the Thunderstrike Diaries

Tensions between the raider group Outlier Action and the Human Collective Administration are ramping up.  And now a new pressure group called False Manifesto has appeared.

Presidential elections are only a Standard away, and unpopular Collective President Klas Jorrak is determined to cling onto power.  He is opposed by popular candidate Bryssa Meir, who is endorsed by False Manifesto.

Strike, the sapient machine intelligence of *Thunderstrike*, is searching for the Vatan sisters.  Now he hears rumours that the President has ordered the sisters' assassination.   Then Strike receives video of a False Manifesto rally, and he suspects that one of the women on the stage there is Merrill Vatan.

As False Manifesto demonstrations are violently disrupted and their members murdered, Strike sends Snap and Bahar to find the woman.  Can they find Merrill and take her to safety before she becomes the next victim?

# HONESTY POLICY

## Book 5 of the Thunderstrike Diaries

With the Presidential election growing near, a new pressure group, Sister Strategy, joins the fray. Strike, the machine intelligence of the frigate *Thunderstrike*, is on the lookout for the last Vatan sister, Nyla. And he thinks he's spotted her at a Sister Strategy rally.

When Presidential candidate Bryssa Meir is bitten by a dog and poisoned, Strike discovers that President Jorrak has started another illegal project. Now he's trying to turn dogs into Predatorbots.

After Strike briefly spots Nyla at another rally, she disappears. When he picks up her trail again, she is headed for Central Station. Strike is forced to follow her there.

But at Central Station the risks of his illegal Special Investigations Unit being discovered are high.

Can Strike keep Nyla safe without endangering himself?